A HAUNT FOR OWLS

Brother Adam!
Keep spreading the Good News!
MATT POSEY

A HAUNT FOR OWLS

MATT POSEY

Published by Redemption Press Express, 1602 Cole Street, Enumclaw, WA 98022, (360) 226-3488.

Redemption Press Express is honored to present this title in partnership with the author. The views expressed or implied in this work are those of the author. Redemption Press Express provides our imprint seal representing design excellence, creative content, and high-quality production. This is a work of fiction. Names, characters, businesses, places, events, and incidents in this book are either the products of the author's imagination or used in a fictitious manner. Any resemblance to actual persons, living or dead, or actual events is purely coincidental.

ISBN 13: 978-1-64645-696-3 (paperback)

978-1-64645-699-4 (ePub)

Library of Congress Catalog Card Number: 2024914452

To the one true God, who took a simple conversation
between friends and turned it into a
message of his redemption.

It will lie desolate; no one will ever pass through it again
... [it] will become a haunt for jackals, a home for owls.

Isaiah 34:10, 13 NIV

PART I
DESOLATION

THERE IS A WAY THAT SEEMS RIGHT TO A MAN, BUT ITS
END IS THE WAY TO DEATH.
PROVERBS 14:12
(ESV)

Prologue

Indian Territory
Winter 1864

Private Doyle Hill stood watch near the edge of his little outpost. Things were quiet. Normally, quiet was good, but this was a different kind of quiet. First, it was an eerie quiet—a before-the-storm quiet. Second, it was unexpected. Under Captain Jacob Feral's orders, Doyle's Confederate outpost had recently intercepted a Yankee supply wagon, taking all they could and burning the rest. Retaliation would come, Feral promised, and this morning's fog was the perfect cover for mounting an offensive.

Doyle breathed out a long, slow cloud of fog into the frosty February air and peered into the mist. Maybe he was wrong about today. After all, there were at least as many reasons against mounting an offensive as there were for it. But then, there was that insufferable silence in which he could find no peace—oppressive, suffocating, and somehow deafening.

In an instant, the mist cleared all the way to the far hill, and Doyle saw with horror the deadly howitzers, prepared by the enemy to visit all of God's wrathful brimstone upon their heads.

"Contact!" he screamed.

And all hell broke loose.

Confused shouts went up among the rebel soldiers amid the sudden crackle of musket fire and the *whoosh* of incoming lead.

"Form ranks!" Feral shouted.

He began shoving men into formation, trying to create some semblance of a picket line.

"Form! Ranks!"

Doyle remained at his post, away from the picket line, gripping his musket and silently pleading with himself to obey Feral's inevitable order to charge.

"Fix bayonets!" Feral yelled.

Doyle tried to control the shaking of his hands. His hands were strong, lean, and hard knuckled, but they wouldn't help him, shaking as they were.

Feral grabbed Doyle by the shoulder and screamed.

"Hill! Move! *Move*!"

Doyle's lips formed an echo.

"Move," he mouthed to himself. "Move!"

He had feared this day and what it would bring. No man knows how he will react in a crisis until he is neck deep in it, but Doyle was a practical man and knew himself better than most men know themselves. Since the Confederacy had pressed him into service, he had been afraid—of death and injury, yes, but even more afraid of what might happen next—

Whoosh! BOOM!

Doyle's ears filled with ringing. Everyone hit the ground. Several, including Doyle, didn't get back up. Feral abandoned Doyle and began shouting about the twelve-pounders on the far hill. It was a silly warning. First, no one could hear it; second, no one needed it. Feral raised his musket and tried to fire, but it failed to discharge. The cartridge was bad. Cursing, he threw the useless gun on the grass and grabbed another from one of the fallen men.

The battle intensified. Doyle could not will himself to action and no longer tried. His senses took everything in—the explosions and screams, the smoke from gunfire—and packed it all into his addled brain.

"Where is the boy?" someone shouted. Doyle knew they were referring to Private Harper.

Rodney Harper was the seventeen-year-old drummer, assistant, burial detail, and latrine maintainer, who additionally served as the company's battlefield medic in times such as this. The "boy" was nowhere to be found. Sergeant Johnson, too, was missing.

"Put some fire on that hillside!" Feral screamed in between shell explosions.

Private Caskill dropped to one knee and did his best to return some lead to the cannon crews on the hill. A musket ball shattered his leg just below the knee, putting him out of action. Filmore was down as well, clutching his shrapnel-shredded face in his hands and screaming.

Whoosh! BOOM!

Feral raised the musket to his shoulder, but before he could fire, his head snapped back, and the gun flew from his hands. He hit the ground hard, his remaining eye staring lifelessly at the frozen Private Doyle Hill.

It was evident from the start that the Union force would carry the victory, and the rebels now began to fall back toward the larger camp to the south. Doyle continued to sit, catatonic, a dead man breathing, waiting for bullets and shrapnel to tear into him. The lull in gunfire barely registered in his mind.

"Doyle!"

"Hill!"

Doyle blinked. Someone was calling to him, telling him to move. *Move!* he told himself silently. He couldn't do it.

For now, still outside the effective range of musket fire, the Yankees continued to advance, carefully and methodically, toward Doyle's position.

"Come on. We have to move!"

It was Harper! Harper, the hapless, toilet-cleaning whipping boy. Doyle's breath quickened.

Harper put a hand on Doyle's shoulder and shook him. Doyle blinked again and tried to focus his eyes as if shaking off a nightmare. Age notwithstanding, Harper was big—and he'd never looked bigger or stronger than he did right now.

The shouts of the Yankees grew closer. Without another word, Private Harper folded Doyle over his shoulder and ran for both their lives.

CHAPTER ONE

Potatoes

Northwest Nevada
Fall 1873

Doyle Hill opened the small corral where his cattle spent their nights. The little herd trickled out of the enclosure, and Doyle, mounted on horseback, held back the two cows that produced milk for the ranch workers—all three of them, including Doyle.

Back in Texas, the place would never pass as a ranch, but out here in the high desert, well, it was the best any three people could manage. Besides Doyle, there was Harper—Doyle's business partner and friend—and there was his wife, Annie, who would eventually milk the last two cows and turn them out to join the rest of the herd.

Doyle, though no longer a private by rank, was deeply private by nature. For this reason, he enjoyed ranging the cattle in the early mornings while Annie attended to her domestics in the cabin they shared. Harper, who despised frigid mornings, wouldn't turn out of his little hut for another hour.

Right on his own time, about midmorning, Harper trotted his horse out to join Doyle, driving a few straggling cows back to the larger herd as he went.

"Little early today, you reckon?" Harper said.

"Only for some," Doyle responded.

"Only for honest men," Harper corrected. "No one does good deeds in the dark." He shivered. "It is too cold out here, Hill."

Doyle gave Harper a sideways glance. He never understood how anyone Harper's size could ever feel cold. Not that he was overweight by any stretch, but surely his whiskey-barrel chest and matching arms had to provide some insulation. Doyle was tall and strong but had little weight to spare. Even so, he was only twenty pounds less capable than any man with fifty pounds over him.

"You should wake earlier and warm up with some of Annie's coffee," Doyle said.

"Coffee is for those who get up earlier than they should."

"Maybe some warm milk, then."

Doyle cracked a smile and Harper couldn't help a snicker. Then, as quickly as it surfaced, the humor was gone again. This was their way; simple, easy, and only as deep as necessary to keep their friendship alive.

Doyle straightened in the saddle and looked toward his cabin. It was midmorning, and the hundred-and-fifty-yard view was clear. Annie stood in the yard. Someone was approaching her. It was a man on horseback, pulling a cart.

"This cannot be good," Doyle muttered.

Ever distrustful, Doyle began to imagine any number of sinister reasons a man with a cart would approach a lone woman outside her cabin—not the least of which was pure prejudice: Annie's skin color. There was also the fact that Doyle and Harper served in the Confederacy yet now claimed prize access to the river in what had been Union territory. Doyle, Harper, and Annie were about as unwelcome as any three people could be, and this was something on which Doyle dwelt too much.

"Hyah!"

Doyle took off at a gallop. Harper, clearly surprised by Doyle's sudden reaction, made a quick check of the herd and followed.

Doyle slowed his gallop as he approached the house. There was no sense in riding in like a cavalry charge. He did, however, untie the leather straps that secured his Colt in its holster. Not that he'd likely need it—or even be able to bring himself to use it if he did—but, somehow, it made him feel a little more prepared. There was also the added benefit of sending a silent message. No one untied their holster straps except in polite threat.

He dismounted and approached Annie, who stood in conversation with the visiting gentleman.

"It is very kind. Thank you," she told the stranger.

"Think nothing of it, ma'am. Happy to help a neighbor."

The man turned his attention to Doyle, who had parked himself beside Annie. "You must be Mr. Hill."

"I am."

"Mr. Hill, my name is Stanford Campbell. I am the foreman at the Sutton Ranch just up the way."

Doyle nodded his acknowledgment. "Doyle Hill," he said.

Campbell walked over to his cart, and Doyle looked at Annie.

"What is his business?" he asked her quietly.

"Potatoes," said Annie.

"Pota—!"

Doyle caught himself mid-word. His hand dropped to cover his revolver, and he began scouring the area for threats.

Where? he thought frantically.

He moved in front of Annie, separating her from Campbell, the copse of trees to the north, and the road to the east.

Years ago, Doyle and Annie had developed a short list of cipher words to use in case of trouble. *Potatoes*, in this context, indicated a suspected ambush.

Why is she so calm? he wondered.

Annie seemed to suddenly remember the double meaning of *potato* and placed her hand on Doyle's arm.

"Look," she said and pointed.

Campbell slid two giant gunnysacks from his cart and placed them on the ground. They fairly burst at the seams.

"We had a bumper potato crop this year," he said. "More than our cellars can hold. Mr. Sutton asked me to bring these two sacks to you."

"Why us?" Doyle said.

Annie squeezed his arm, reminding him to be neighborly.

"Goodwill, I suppose," Campbell answered. "Never a bad idea

to bless a neighbor—particularly a close neighbor. These bags are heavy." He grinned.

By this time, Harper had ridden up. He took one look at the sacks.

"Potatoes?" he guessed.

Doyle made a slight sweep of his palm as if to say, "Stay out of it, Rod."

"How much would you like for them?" Doyle asked Campbell.

"They are a gift," Campbell replied.

Doyle swallowed, and Annie grimaced. Doyle didn't accept gifts, and she knew it.

"It is generous of you," Doyle said. "Too generous. Allow me to pay you."

"Sutton wants you to have them, Mr. Hill."

Doyle didn't bite. He'd place himself in no one's debt.

"I cannot accept. I need potatoes this winter and have planned to purchase them in town this week. Delivering them to me is gift enough, thank you."

He turned to Harper.

"Take a side of beef from the smokehouse and give it to Mr. Campbell."

Harper obeyed, and the reluctant Campbell returned to his boss.

An hour later, Doyle and Harper, having dressed up the wandering herd, once again parked alongside each other.

"I do not understand why you did not accept the potatoes," Harper complained. "We need them—and we needed the beef."

"Never accept a gift from a wealthier man, you will always end up in his pocket." Doyle turned to his younger friend to see if he understood. "We will slaughter one more during the winter if needed."

That evening, Doyle sat down to the thick soup his wife had prepared.

"No Harper tonight?" he asked.

"He wanted to take his meal in his home," Annie answered. "He is becoming solitary."

"He has always been despondent now and again," Doyle replied.

"I worry about the man. Has he said anything to you?"

"No."

"Have you said anything to him?" Annie shot back.

"There is nothing to say. If something is bothering him, then he will let me know. Otherwise, it is just moodiness, and it will pass."

"Have you thought about what I said?"

Annie was clearly driving at something. "What did you say earlier?"

Annie shot him a fleeting glare. "I know you feel indebted to him, Doyle, but maybe the best way to pay up is to let him seek his fortune elsewhere."

Doyle *had* considered the idea. "I think that would be worse for him. Harper is a follower."

"I know," she conceded. "He may feel abandoned. It is too bad that one so capable is also so incapable. We are richer for him, but he may be the poorer for us. Even so, I think you should spend more time with him."

Perfect Annie. Naive Annie. Annie, who always sought to build and deepen relationships—always at the expense of his comfort.

He changed the subject.

"What herbs have you been growing? I do not know these, but it is very good."

"It should be," Annie said. "It is made from the most expensive potatoes in the country."

Doyle stopped the spoon midway between bowl and mouth.

"But," she continued, "it would have been better with beef."

Doyle wiped his mouth, lowered his spoon, and looked at his wife.

"Annie, unexpected gifts from others are not to be trusted. Besides that, there is great value in self-sufficiency."

"It was that thinking that almost killed us in sixty-seven, Doyle."

Eighteen sixty-seven. Their second winter here had indeed almost killed them. They had been unsettled, had no resources, and had only crude shelters. Borrowing from neighboring homesteaders would have been the wise thing to do, but Doyle would have none of it, and Harper would always follow Doyle's lead. After emerging gaunt and hungry the following spring, Doyle had learned a valuable lesson in preparation, and Annie had learned a lesson in the hardship of pride.

Doyle set down his spoon. Annie was reminding him of his failure and it made him angry.

"I did what I did, Annie. I cannot take it back, but this—" he indicated the soup "—this is different. We are not starving to death, looking for silver where there is none. We are doing well enough, and there is no sense in looking for generosity where there is none."

"Who cares if it is true generosity or not?" Annie flared. "It is community at least—even if it involves bartering favors."

"It is politics, Annie, and all that means is that someone is going to come out on top—at the expense of others."

"Maybe you will come out on top, Doyle, at the expense of no one. We left the Indian Territory for gold, did we not?"

"We did. And what happened? I know what happened. It was the greedy, murderous, squabbling horde that kept us from moving all the way to California. Everyone scrambling to the top of Gold Mountain, and happy to kill to get there."

"Yes, but not you, Doyle. You would never climb to the top like that."

"That is true ... so we looked for silver here—and almost starved to death," Doyle said.

"Yes, we *almost* starved," said Annie. "And yes, there was no silver to be found, which is not your fault. But you have built a life here for us by doing what you know. Perhaps the only thing missing is a little faith in others. It is the missing beef in your potato soup, my love, that keeps you from the top."

Beautiful, perfect, naive Annie.

CHAPTER TWO

The Nightmare and the Owl

"Wait, please!"

In the frigid air, the rasp could be seen better than heard, but to Doyle Hill, it may as well have been a locomotive's roar. The dying man's lips worked to form words.

"Hill! Do not leave!"

He was posturing for death.

"Come baaaAAACK!" The last word stretched grotesquely into a screech that seemed to last for minutes on end.

Doyle's eyes snapped open, and he drew in sharply. Everything was quiet and dark. Carefully, he moved to a sitting position and wiped the nightmare from his face with both hands.

This wasn't the first time Doyle had dreamed about Private Caskill. In fact, almost a decade had passed since the massacre that stole so much more than his sleep. Private Caskill. The man Doyle had abandoned on the battlefield. Private Caskill, whose stiff corpse

Doyle and Harper had loaded onto a death cart. The real Private Caskill had been left with less than lethal wounds, only to have his throat cut by Union forces under orders to "take no prisoners." That wasn't how the dream played out, though.

He slid his hand softly to his left. She was still there, still asleep. Annie, too, had her demons, but at least she seemed to sleep well.

Doyle had met Annie at the tail end of the war; widowed, orphaned, and educated by experience in the primal brutality of man. She had been shattered yet had somehow put herself back together in a way most would consider impossible. Annie was beautiful—simply beautiful—though not in the basic way the term implied. She was pretty, yes, but it was the simplicity of her manner—unassuming, genuine, and free—that made her so perfect. At least, that was what appealed to Doyle. He wasn't particularly smitten at first; he merely saw her as she was, even if everyone else was blind to it.

"I am Doyle," he had said.

"Annie," she'd returned.

"That is your school name?"

Doyle had assumed that, like most Choctaw Indians in the territories, Annie had been given an Anglo name upon entering school.

"It is. My true name is Nita." Then, though she would admit later that she didn't know why, she added, "It means bear."

Doyle couldn't help a smile. There was nothing bear-like about the little woman before him.

"Which do you prefer, ma'am?" Doyle asked.

"You may call me Annie. I am used to it."

Their wedding followed soon after, although it was more a

"prairie arrangement" than a wedding—official, but not joyous. Two broken people who, after the devastation of war, had nothing to pick up but themselves, instead agreed to pick up each other and start life over. There was no love between them that day, but there was a kindness to it.

On the night of their wedding, they were preparing for the awkward duty of consummating their union when Annie began to sob. Doyle approached her carefully.

"Please, I will not touch you tonight," he said.

Annie cried harder, and as her shoulders shook, Doyle saw, for the first time, the scars that marred the soft skin of her shoulders and back.

"I am sorry, Mr. Hill!"

Doyle was perplexed. "What are you sorry for?"

Annie drew in a deep breath in several long gasps. "I-I should have ... told you before. It just happened so fast."

Doyle wondered what type of hammer was about to fall. Perhaps she belonged to another man, or possibly she had lost her nerve and would now leave him.

"I cannot bear you children," she said.

Her face collapsed into her hands, and shame poured from her eyes.

Doyle longed for words that would make it better, but none came. He was a kind man, and wise enough to know that sharing his philosophy on bringing new life into such a hateful world was the last thing a barren woman would want to hear.

He caressed her shoulders, comfortingly and without agenda, and said, "I will still be yours."

Doyle's new wife's sobs gradually subsided. His fingers absently worked over her scars for a few minutes before he caught himself.

"Annie. Who did this to you?"

She looked up at him for a moment. "Angry men."

She traced her fingers from her husband's ear, down his neck, and to his chest. She followed the markings across his shoulders, so like her own.

"Who did this to you?" she whispered.

"Evil men."

That night, Doyle and Annie held each other in the first real comfort they had enjoyed in many years.

And there they were, seven years later, seventeen hundred miles away, belonging to each other in a way neither of them had expected.

If the screech in his dreams had interrupted his slumber, the screech outside the cabin nearly stopped his heart. In a moment, it turned the night inside out so that the resuming silence now became deafening. He recovered, marveling that Annie did not wake. Doyle stood up and pulled on his pants. Seven years he'd been here. He'd built every structure and made every improvement. He, Annie, and Harper had carved out a life. He'd seen, smelled, and heard everything there was to this land, but never this. He was awake now.

Doyle quietly moved from the bedroom to the window at the front of the house. He stared for a few minutes before opening the door and stepping out onto the weathered porch. His toes curled over the warped boards as he strained his eyes into the night and began to doubt his senses. It was real, was it not? Was it just in his—

There! Maybe ten yards away. Two close-set eyes intensely reflected the meager moonlight. Unwavering. Staring him down, giving him an unearthly feeling.

For almost a minute, Doyle stared back. It scared him, and he hated that. He urged himself to bend down and wrap his fingers around a solid stick of firewood beside him. Doyle was a practical man, and even in this state, it occurred to him how low the wood stack had already become. This winter was going to be tough. He stood up, cocked back, and whipped the club through the air. The bird scrambled awkwardly into the sky, and Doyle immediately lost sight of it. He breathed out heavily and looked toward Harper's hut. It was dark and still. Not that Doyle had expected him to stir. It was a joke as old as their friendship that Harper could sleep through anything.

During the war, Doyle and several other men in his army unit had awoken one night to a raiding band of natives attempting to rustle horses while the men slept. It was a fool move, stealing horses from armed men, but times had been desperate. Harper had just been wriggling out of his bedroll as the last of the bandits dispersed. It had taken gunfire to rouse him.

"Fool! Boy!" Furious, Captain Feral had stormed over to the thrashing young private and screamed. "Will ... only ... a ... bullet ... teach ... you?"

Each word had been punctuated by a sharp kick to the ribs, stomach, and legs. Feral had been right about one thing, Harper had been a boy—barely seventeen at the time. His age, however, had done nothing to hamper the satisfaction of the men who felt that Harper's inaction had put them in danger.

Over the next two days, Doyle saved half his rations for the bruised Harper. As if the beating wasn't enough, Harper was denied meals as punishment for his sloth.

"I wish a bullet would teach the captain," Harper told Doyle.

"Let it go," Doyle said, "Feral is the commanding officer. He is responsible for good order and discipline. You do not have to like him, but being disrespectful will get you more than beaten."

"He is a fool," Harper said.

"Enough. Your actions have no defense. Whether or not Feral's discipline was fair is a different matter altogether. You need to let this go."

Doyle was right, but, despite his kindness, his words (and Harper's reaction to them) put their budding friendship on rough terrain until Harper's pride scabbed over.

Now, Doyle stood outside the cabin a few minutes longer, scanning the darkness for any sign of the owl's return, then loaded an arm with kindling. Nothing for it now. He turned back to the house. He'd stoke the fire and try to enjoy the quiet before dawn. This had been a hateful way to wake up, and there was no more sleep to be had tonight.

Annie awoke to an empty bed and saw her husband's silhouette flickering in the light of the small fire. She went out to him.

"It was another dream?" she said.

Doyle nodded but did not elaborate.

Annie sat next to him. "What happens to you in the night?"

"It is the same thing every time. Just men killing each other in the war."

"There is more than that, Doyle. Let me help."

"There is nothing more," he said for the hundredth time in a hundred iterations of this same conversation. "It is mine to forget, not yours to remember."

"Sharing with me may help you forget."

Doyle leaned over and kissed her forehead. He loved her. Her desire to help, her love for him, all of her. "I cannot."

And he was right. Annie could not know that he had been a coward in the field of battle; that instead of pulling Caskill to safety, Harper had been forced to rescue Doyle. Caskill had died due to Doyle's inaction. Nor could he tell her about the owl outside the house.

Annie hated owls.

In the darkness of Doyle's reticence, Annie consoled herself by getting up, crossing over to the little kitchen, and beginning preparations for an unusually lavish breakfast. It wasn't much, but it was something—something she could control—and it made her feel better.

CHAPTER THREE

Unwelcome News

Later that morning, Doyle and Harper cut logs by the river on the west end of their claim. The cattle seemed content to stay in the area, which allowed the two men a rare opportunity to range the cattle, perform a necessary chore, and remain in each other's company. The whole operation of their outfit was not terribly efficient. They relied on some natural barriers to encourage the herd to stay local, driving them out farther to range only as necessary. This worked as the herd was still fairly small.

They had discussed fencing last year—that was, Annie had suggested it, and Doyle was dead set against it. Fences were an expensive endeavor and wouldn't eliminate the need for cattle driving in the winter months when the landscape went dormant. Nor would it keep the herd from simply pushing the fence over by whim or accident. Lastly, though his practicality made Doyle loathe to admit it, fencing was for farmers. He and Harper were cowboys.

"I never thought I would meet an Indian in favor of a fence," Harper had observed.

"When was the last time you saw Annie in anything besides a cotton dress?" Doyle had retorted. "She is a farmer. Farmers like fences."

Back in the unfenced field, Doyle dragged a load of thick branches over to where Harper was chopping and splitting logs.

"You hear the owl last night?"

Harper looked up questioningly. "No ... never in these parts."

Of course he hadn't.

"I suppose it could have nested in your hut and screamed all night without you knowing," Doyle said.

Harper scoffed. "I know it did not wake you, Hill. You would have to be *asleep* for that."

Doyle ignored him. Doyle's insomnia was no secret.

"Did the missus wake?" Harper asked.

"No."

"Perhaps you did sleep and dreamed it all."

"It was real. He was not thirty feet away, and I almost took off his head."

Harper took his attention from the axe in his hand. He was interested now. He paused, looking toward the house. "Nothing good comes of owls."

Doyle huffed.

Nothing good comes from superstition, he thought, *and now I have spooked Harper*.

Doyle wished he'd kept the whole thing to himself. God help him if Annie found out.

"Nothing good for the owl," he said as if to dismiss Harper's fears. "If I see him again, I will shoot him."

Harper swung hard and then cursed. The axe handle had splintered, sending a bone-shaking shock through his hands. He clenched his fists and pretended to check the herd. Composing himself, he picked up the axe-head and kicked the broken handle away.

"What is this dry-rot stuff anyway?" he said. "What I would give for some hickory in this god-forsaken place."

Doyle grinned to himself. Harper's impetuous temper almost always amused him, although he himself would have been intensely frustrated had the axe broken on any other day. As it was, a trip into town had to be made soon, and this was a good reason to make the trip a day or two early.

"Looks like we are heading to Weston, today," Doyle said.

Harper attempted to remove the splinters from inside the axe-head. "This late in the morning?"

"You have another axe?"

Harper's face answered the question. "I could make the trip alone," he suggested.

The arrival of the Central Pacific Railroad a few years prior had caused the little post of Weston to blossom into a veritable retail oasis almost overnight. Local homesteaders now enjoyed easy access to necessaries, which had previously required a much longer journey to secure. Doyle, who generally disliked community, wasn't particularly keen on Weston's rapid growth but had to admit that trading three-day wagon drives for day trips had been a boon for his little ranch. With any luck, he and Harper could return before nightfall.

"I will go," Doyle said. "You cannot carry everything on old Clyde, and two horses are faster than the wagon."

"Annie may want to go," said Harper. "In that case, we will need the wagon anyway."

Doyle grimaced. The wagon was slow. True, he could just send Annie with Harper, but he didn't like sending Annie into town unless he accompanied her. Not that Harper wouldn't watch out for her, but he liked the saloon, and Annie did not. She was likely to leave Harper to go shopping alone—and unprotected.

A few minutes later, Doyle dismounted next to the garden and approached his wife. She was on her knees, pulling the last of her greens, and had not seen him coming. Doyle leaned over her and playfully pinched her sides. Annie let out a startled "yip" and pretended to stab at her husband with her gardening knife.

"You will regret that one day, Hill," she said.

"I believe you," he said. "You are handier with a knife than any man I have seen."

"What do you want? Besides your own death?"

"Harper broke the axe. We have to go into town and will pick up the last few items we need before winter."

"He is too forceful with things."

"He is just strong. Even so, we need to finish cutting the logs on the west end soon. We need to go today. Should I round up the critters?"

"Leave them. I will stay and pen them up when I finish with

this." She pointed at the remaining greens with her knife.

Doyle and Harper reached Weston without event and stabled their horses. As they approached the train depot near the heart of the city, the broad-chested Harper struggled against the crowd to keep up with the lankier, nimbler Doyle.

"This place doubles in size every time I come here," Doyle muttered, mostly to himself. Truthfully, he wasn't that far off.

The two men made their way to the general store and quickly filled their order.

As the storekeeper's assistant packed their sundries, Harper turned to Doyle. "You mind me perusing a bit before heading back?"

Doyle clenched his jaw. He'd known this was coming, but he had still entertained hope for an early escape back into solitude. Harper had his own needs, and it would likely be a couple of months before they came back. He decided not to argue.

"Why not peruse yourself up a wife?" said Doyle.

Harper grinned and looked down the street as though to identify a suitable candidate.

"I suppose I could ... although ..." He pretended to strain his eyes before concluding, with mock superiority. "I see no one suitable to my standards."

"It is just as well. She would not approve of your sod, and you would be forced to build a house."

"That is true. I will stick to the whiskey, then."

Harper made his way toward the saloon, leaving Doyle to suffer the unpleasantness of the bustle around him.

There was an energy today that Doyle disliked—beyond his own social aversion. He mentally inventoried the day's purchases to determine if there was anything else he needed to pick up. As he walked, Doyle noticed that the conversations on the street had become serious in nature. Men spoke in grave tones, and women whispered to each other by the storefronts.

Nothing good comes of whispers.

Yes, there was something in the air, something like fear. Doyle looked up and found he had arrived in front of the saloon. He stood for some minutes, wondering whether he should go in.

Maybe the air is lighter inside. He still felt the oppressive atmosphere of the street. Perhaps he could find out what was going on. Perhaps he could find Harper and drag him home.

"If you have to think that hard about it, perhaps you should leave it alone."

The voice startled Doyle from his thoughts. He turned, immediately recognizing the speaker as a man of the cloth. Doyle was instantly annoyed. Why else would a preacher talk to him if not to turn him from his sinful ways? Doyle tolerated authority just enough to be left alone; otherwise, he made his own rules.

"Maybe you should join me." He nodded at the saloon.

The minister grinned good-naturedly.

"No?" Doyle asked.

"No," came the reply.

"Probably for the best," Doyle pretended to conclude. "I suppose God would not approve."

"God takes no issue with a little whiskey," said the cleric cautiously. "I abstain for others' sake."

Doyle wasn't sure why or what, but there was something he kind of liked about this man. Maybe because he was different than the other preachers he'd met. Doyle wasn't purposely cynical, but it was strange to hear a preacher say there was something God didn't condemn.

Doyle's curiosity overcame his aloofness. "Whose sake, then?"

The man seemed first to consider whether he'd said too much. Then, as if deciding Doyle could be trusted to understand, he gestured to everyone around them. Doyle chewed on this for a moment, and the preacher clarified.

"You assume me to be temperate. So do they. If their assumptions cannot be changed, it is better for me to abstain than for them to think I condone sin."

This was something new to Doyle. To obey a law and thereby escape punishment was natural, but to limit oneself simply for the benefit of another's conscience—the whole thing tasted bad.

"Seems to me a man ought to do what he feels is right, and let others do the same."

There. He'd said it. A few silent moments passed between the two men. Doyle had almost decided to walk away when the man responded.

"Has that worked for you?"

It wasn't rude, but it was pointed.

"Well enough, I suppose," Doyle said.

"What happens when two men disagree on what is right?"

Doyle looked around for an escape from the conversation. Seeing none, he answered. "I suppose one of them is lying to himself then."

The preacher stroked his stubbled chin. "What if there is only one—ever—who is right?"

Doyle smiled uncomfortably. "You mean God?"

The man smiled. "You said it, not me."

Doyle's patience was waning. "If God is right, then I think he would have made the world a little more right as well."

"Reverend Camber!"

Across the street, a man was hailing the preacher.

"I like you, Mr. Hill. Hope to see you again soon."

Doyle touched his hat and watched his acquaintance hurry across to the waiting parishioner. It bothered him that Camber knew his name. What else did Camber know about him? That he had fought for the rebels? That he was a coward? Doyle pushed the unpleasant thought away. If nothing else, Camber seemed a decent man—for a preacher.

Several men walked hastily in the direction of the town square. Doyle recognized one of them as Henry Schutz, the sheriff. Something was definitely wrong.

A hand on his shoulder made him start; he quickly turned to see Harper standing behind him.

"You ready?" Harper's expression was grim. "This place is making me uneasy."

So, Harper had picked up on it too.

Doyle and Harper headed back to the store to load up their order and found John, the owner, locking the door.

"You are just in time," he said, quickly unlocking the door. "Wait here a moment—everything is packaged up."

After watching the clerk make a few frenetic trips to and from the back room, Harper lost patience.

"What is going on?" he blurted.

Thank God, Doyle thought, *somebody had to ask*.

John looked incredulously from man to man. "There was a murder at the Stanley homestead. About a half day's ride north from here."

Seeing no sign of recognition from either man, John continued. "The whole family. Killed. Indian raid, I expect. Terrible stuff. Schutz has asked for a dozen men to assist in the investigation, and I have agreed to help."

The news weighed on Doyle. Indian raids weren't unheard of in these parts, but they were almost always preceded by dispute and could be easily traced back to the source. At least, that was Doyle's personal experience.

Shortly before the war had put a stop to Doyle's cattle driving career, he and eleven other men had been driving a herd through Indian Territory. Jose, the trail boss, began the customary negotiations with local tribe leaders as the group moved through the Indian Territories. Jose was shrewd, but so were the natives.

One evening, Jose motioned for Jeb—his "segundo"—and Doyle to move from their point positions to the head of the herd.

"A hundred head!" Jose shouted. "A hundred! Last spring, we passed through for twenty!"

Jeb spat.

"Sounds like that is the price, jefe," Jeb said.

"Extortion is what it is. If word of this spreads, there will be nothing left for us in Kansas City."

This was Doyle's fourth drive with the outfit, which made him Jose and Jeb's most senior cowboy. On this drive, both men had begun to confide in him when it came to management matters. Doyle knew he had no positional authority, but he cherished the mutual trust among the three of them. He would ride through the gates of hell with them.

"This has to stop," Jose said.

"What do you propose, boss?" Doyle asked. "Double-cross a nation and we are likely to lose twelve more heads."

"I have been negotiating for years, Hill. Have a little faith in my abilities."

"I do not doubt your ability, boss, but the deal is done."

Jose swung around to face Doyle. "Maybe it is, and maybe it is not. Either way, it is my decision."

"Yes sir."

"Have I ever let you down?"

"No sir."

"Have I ever had to pay you less than agreed because of expenses incurred on the trail?"

Doyle shook his head. "No sir."

"I need you to trust me, then. Completely."

"I did not mean to say I thought you would cheat the Indians," Doyle protested.

Jeb dismissed the apology on Jose's behalf with a wave of his hand. "We know you meant nothing by it."

Jose smiled graciously, and the three men moved toward their posts at the front of the herd, which had continued past them during the parley.

Doyle trotted a little closer to Jose. "I do trust you ... completely. You are a good man, Jefe."

Jose winked and touched his hat. All was good between them.

The following morning, the bosses woke the crew several hours before first light.

"Head 'em up! Move 'em out!"

Doyle looked around. Some of the junior cowboys were missing.

"Where is Jimenez? Greaves? And—"

"They are ahead of us," Jeb answered. "We need to move before we fall too far behind."

"You should have roused me first." Doyle threw together his bedroll.

Jeb urged the crew to move the herd double-time while Jose rode up front. Doyle began feeling uneasy.

"Trust me," Jose had said, "completely," and Doyle had vowed to do just that. Jose was shrewd, but he was a good man. However, Doyle had to double his resolve when the four missing cowboys joined them, not from the front as Jeb had led him to believe, but from the rear—and with roughly seventy-five longhorn cattle.

They wandered, that is all, he told himself. *Jose sent the men back for them.*

Truthfully, that made more sense than the alternative theory that somehow Jose had rustled back what he thought was unfair. First of all, Jose had to move five thousand longhorns out of range before the tribe discovered the theft. Secondly, negotiations with Native Americans and farmers were critical to the trade. Burn bridges now, and any future drives would be out of the question. Doyle knew this because Jeb and Jose had taught him. They were career men.

All at once, a rifle cracked. Then another, then another. Doyle turned to see Jose shouting at the men.

"Move!"

The herd spooked and began to stampede. Dust rose amid the thundering hooves, frantic shouts, and gunfire. Unable to see or move toward the boss men, Doyle first steered clear of the panicked herd, then dropped back to find Greaves and Smith, who occupied the swing and flank positions on Doyle's side.

After a few minutes, he found Smith, wide-eyed, his head on a swivel.

"What happened?" Doyle yelled above the roar.

Smith could only curse.

"Hey!" Doyle yelled.

Smith looked at Doyle, seemingly without recognition.

Doyle looked Smith in the face. "Draw your iron!"

Smith pulled his Colt Dragoon and continued to look wildly around.

Greaves joined them from the rear, reins in one hand, rifle in the other.

"What is it?" Doyle asked.

"Injuns! They are back for their property ... and for blood!"

"What?"

It made no sense. Risking everything for a few dozen cows? He leaned in toward Greaves. "Why did you do it?"

"Jefe's orders, Hill, and double my take in Kansas City."

Smith was slowly coming to his senses. "We were supposed to be safe once we crossed into Kansas."

Doyle motioned to the others.

"We cannot stay h—"

Boom!

Adrenaline and fear propelled Doyle around just as Smith fell out of his saddle.

"Move!" Doyle yelled.

He and Greaves galloped hard, trying to get in front of the herd and looking for comrades who were already dead.

Taking fire from every direction, Doyle and Greaves abandoned their horses and lay down in the tall grass with their weapons. Doyle hoped the Indians would be content to steal the entire herd and leave.

His hopes were quickly dashed. The marauders knew how many men were on the trail—and how many survivors it would take to alert the US Army. Recognizing that capture was imminent, Greaves committed himself to their mercy.

"Over here!" he called, holding his hands up in surrender.

There was a "Whoop!" and a single gunshot. Greaves's body landed next to Doyle, who returned fire with his musket. Greaves's killer fell. Ten yards away, the warrior's companion swung his gun toward the white man. Doyle, who had no prayer of reloading his musket, clenched his eyes shut, waiting for death.

The gun emitted a disappointed "click," and both men opened their eyes. Doyle's assailant drew a knife. Doyle reached for his Colt but only felt the holster. The gun had fallen out during his flight. The two men clashed, knife against flesh, knuckles against face. Completely unarmed, Doyle fought his attacker with pure adrenaline.

In the end, the knife won. Bleeding profusely from the neck, Doyle dropped to the ground. The warrior, believing he had dealt a lethal wound, stabbed Doyle several times in the shoulder and back for good measure before finally abandoning the fight. How Doyle survived the next twenty-four hours, he would never know. He would not have seen the next twenty-four had he not been picked up by another outfit—who had dealt honestly with the natives.

In the end, jealous men had cheated greedy men; vengeful men had slaughtered dishonest men. Envy, greed, pride, wrath. All of it was evil.

Now, with John—and likely all of Weston—suggesting an Indian raid, one question burned in Doyle's mind. "Why would they do that? Is there bad blood?"

"Not that I have heard," John admitted, "but all feuds begin somewhere."

Harper shouldered one of the bundles. "We are headed north. Do you need more help?"

Doyle shifted uncomfortably. He should have been the one to offer. As citizens, he and Harper had a duty to offer their services, but the idea of having to raise a gun against a man made his palms sweat. He doubted he'd be able to do it.

John's answer rescued him from his fear.

"Thank you," he responded. "No. Word has spread more than it should, and now we have too many volunteers to be helpful."

Doyle and Harper headed home without a word between them. Doyle knew his dreams would haunt him again tonight, and with no real way to redeem himself from his fear, he soothed himself a little by vowing not to leave Annie unprotected on the homestead again. It made him feel like a protector—like the man he needed to be.

Evil had found him once more.

CHAPTER FOUR

The Legend of Ishkitini

Doyle and Harper arrived to find Annie corralling the herd early. Her worried expression indicated that she knew something was wrong. Even William, the ranch's mutt, seemed a little off. William spent his days trotting among the cattle herd and his nights hunting rats. Today, however, he stuck close to Annie for comfort.

By the time Doyle and Harper had unloaded the supplies into the Hills' cabin—minus the axe, which Harper took down to the log pile—Annie had yelped the last of the cows into the corral and was closing the gate. Doyle rode up to her, partially to indicate his intention to help, and partially to find out what she knew. He didn't have to wait long.

"We had visitors today," she said.

"Who?"

"Two men from Weston. There has been a mur—a massacre. Asa

Stanley, the silver prospector, his wife, and two children. Even their *dog*, Doyle."

"They came from town? Who sent them?"

"The sheriff. He dispatched riders to warn every homestead within a day's ride."

They sat quietly in the saddle for a few moments, both afraid to acknowledge the business and social complications a suspected Indian attack could bring on them.

Doyle put the horses up for the night, then followed Annie into the cabin for dinner. He began to remove and clean his gear while she worked her knife over the Suttons' potatoes.

"It was Lincoln."

Doyle looked up. "What was Lincoln?"

"Mr. Lincoln and his sons found the Stanleys this morning. Lincoln is Sheriff Schutz's cousin, you know ..."

Doyle did not know. Nor did he know how Annie, who spent very little time off the ranch, knew more about his neighbors than he ever cared to learn.

"They were driving a wagon south into Weston," she continued, "and they stopped to call on the Stanleys. They could tell something was wrong even from the road. They called out, and when there was no answer, Mr. Lincoln went to investigate."

She paused as though unsure of her ability to continue. Doyle put down the package he'd been unwrapping and approached Annie, silently encouraging her to go on.

"They were torn to pieces, Doyle. All of them. There was almost nothing left."

Her voice cracked, and Doyle, not sure how to react, let his wife compose herself.

Once she calmed a little, Doyle asked, "What then?"

Annie blinked hard. "He ... he cut the horses from the wagon and had his boys ride into town to report what they found. Once they left, Mr. Lincoln sat in the wagon with his rifle. He watched over things until the sheriff arrived. The crime scene was at least a day old by the time it was discovered."

Doyle didn't buy the theory that the murder came at the hands of Indians, and after Annie's description, he was certain that this was something different. This was unmotivated, an unexplained evil, the stuff of legends. Suddenly, last night's incident with the owl popped into his mind.

He knew what Annie would think if she was aware of last night's visitor. He had first learned of her superstitions shortly after their wedding. One night, before striking out West with Harper, a screech owl had jolted them out of near sleep. Doyle had been surprised at his new bride's visceral reaction to such an identifiable sound.

"It is just an owl," he had whispered. "This cannot be the first you have heard."

He had not meant to sound dismissive. Doyle was kind, but not skilled in soft speech. Although Annie had known Doyle only a matter of weeks, he knew she was aware of his limitations and gave grace to her new husband by explaining rather than reacting.

"I have heard many," she said, "and that is what I find so terrifying."

"You have not become used to it?"

"Coming to expect something is very different than being unafraid of it," she reasoned.

"Why does it frighten you?"

"It is the cry of Ofunlo. He is an omen of death, and he does not lie."

Doyle smiled patronizingly. "It is a superstition ..."

A fire flared behind Annie's eyes. "It is real!"

Doyle opened his mouth, then closed it. He didn't have to be right, but he did need to be a good man; right now, that meant being a good husband, and *that* meant allowing Annie to be Annie—even if she was afraid of legends.

"What does a Foon-low ..."

"Ofunlo."

"Ofunlo," Doyle repeated carefully. "What—whose death does he foretell?"

Annie remained silent.

"Does he also cause the death?" Doyle asked.

Annie rolled over to face him. "He is the messenger. It is Ishkitini who destroys lives."

"Is ... Ishka ... is it also an owl?"

"He is a witch in the form of a horned owl. At night, he becomes a demon and kills."

"How do you stop him?"

"He cannot be stopped," she said.

Now, watching Annie take her anxiety out on the potatoes, Doyle found himself doubly thankful she hadn't heard the owl last night. He had his limits, too, and was already on edge. Right now, he had little patience for her superstitions.

He searched for a way to tell her what the storekeeper had said. He felt he had a duty to warn her.

"People suspect Indians," he began cautiously.

He hated to say it, but he had to. He'd seen enough vigilantism to know that if the case went unsolved, Annie could face persecution.

When she said nothing, he continued. "The sheriff—"

"No!" Annie snapped. "They did not do this! This was not even ... human! Ishk—something—is out there. Until it is gone, we are only safe in the daylight."

Doyle groaned silently. He was more patient than most husbands he'd known, if only because he felt Annie deserved as much. He swallowed and, once again, resolved to give his wife as much grace as he could muster.

"Please, Doyle, if only for my peace."

Doyle tried to ignore the unpleasant realization that the only owl he'd seen in seven years had shown up the very night of this murder—the only murder in seven years.

No, he told himself, *owls do not mean anything, they do not warn people, and they do not turn into demons and slaughter people during the night. It is a meaningless superstition*.

Owl or not, Annie had worked herself into a panicked energy.

"I also want to start fencing the property. We cannot range forever."

What does this have to do with murder? A fence cannot stop anything capable of destroying an entire family.

The very idea repulsed him. A farmer-fence around property

he didn't even own. Like most of the area, it belonged to the government—public land. Land that for several years he had not been eligible to own because of his service in the Confederate army. The pardon issued in 1867 finally gave him the right to apply for title through the Homestead Act, but he could not say how long that would take. It was just another way society had frustrated his attempts to pursue happiness.

Doyle could not understand why Annie was fixating on monsters. How could she—who had suffered so much persecution, violation, and attack only ever at the hands of men—be so quick to blame an evil she'd never seen? He was so tired, and he was losing patience. He snapped.

"Enough!" he erupted, slapping the table.

Annie jumped, and Doyle immediately held up his hand in apology. "Enough," he repeated softly.

He could tell she was hurt, and that made him feel worse. Unable to take it back, he attempted to soften things by explaining what she already knew all too well. "Annie. I know what animals do, and I know what men do. I have never seen a ghost. The only evil out there walks on two legs."

He was angry again at all the desolation caused by comrades and enemies alike, the rape, pillage, and carnage of war, to say nothing of his disappointment in how he'd been treated by his countrymen in the postwar years or the disdain with which his wife was treated.

"They force their will on anyone they can"—his tone was even, but bitter—"take whatever they can, and take pleasure in slaughtering those who do not agree. Monsters all!"

He stared at the table in quiet frustration. His opinion was nothing new to Annie, and he never should have said anything.

Doyle ventured a look up at Annie and was taken aback to see that she was holding back tears. Had he been that cruel?

"And what of me?" she asked quietly. "Will you not forgive? Not even me? Will you remain in your nightmares forever?"

Doyle didn't know how to respond. Somehow, Annie had found peace in extending grace to others. It was naive and childish, and yet it was her innocent and forgiving nature that Doyle loved—and envied—so much. Doyle, on the other hand, believed everyone was evil; the best one could do was try to contain it.

He was not unwilling to trust or forgive, just unable. It was a matter of survival. His life—his *wife*—depended on the protection he provided, a protection that others could never or would never provide.

Even so, he didn't see any bad in Annie. Maybe his love for her made him blind to it. There was no reconciling the matter in his mind, but he couldn't hurt her again. He took her hands tenderly and examined them as if to read her palm.

"Maybe," he said carefully, "not *all* are evil."

Annie touched his cheek. Clearly, she wasn't satisfied. "And what of you, Doyle? I do not know a monster in you."

He was not willing to give any more territory. "It has to be there."

Annie sighed softly in exasperation. "No."

With that, Doyle let the conversation end, silently resolving never to discuss it again. He was a man of simple observations and conclusions; long ago, he had concluded that everyone is evil and should, therefore, not be trusted or submitted to. Like most, he submitted to authority—but only to the extent necessary for survival. When it came to matters of morality, Doyle used his conscience to guide him. It wasn't perfect, but it was simple and had always seemed right to him. Until now.

Annie, in her own gentle way, had challenged his assumptions. He loved her. He loved Harper. That required a measure of trust, didn't it? Could he accept the goodness of those he loved and throw the others out? It felt right, but it didn't figure. What if it wasn't love at all? What if his feelings toward his wife and friend were nothing more than simple survival? The whole thing felt bad. And so, in the manner of many men, Doyle committed himself to putting the whole thing out of mind, as it did not do to dwell on such philosophical luxuries.

That night, Annie lay in bed with her own nightmares. She was seventeen again, full of the same angst she'd experienced earlier in the kitchen with Doyle.

"They should have returned," said Wiyot, a wizened woman in her sixties. She was, in every possible way, a grayer, rounder Annie.

"Peace, *Pokni.* They will return." But Annie's conviction waned.

The screech of Ofunlo had been heard no less than five times—right outside their hut. Both women were on edge.

Annie had been one of the precious few infants to survive the Trail of Tears, and Wiyot had been one of few women over thirty to survive. Her daughter—Annie's mother—and Annie's father didn't make it. Wiyot had cared for her grandchildren ever since.

"It is a white man's war, Nita," Wiyot said. "We have no business supplying either side."

"We will provide it at a cost, or they will take it for free," Annie said.

"They always take, Nita. It is always free."

Tense hours passed before any sign of life was heard in the village that Nita, Wiyot, and seventy-five or so others called home. In a purely capitalist move, one of Annie's brothers had supplied produce to a Union unit. This act violated the treaty the Choctaw nation made with the Confederates, who had, unbeknownst to the village council, determined to make an example of the little community. Annie's husband and brothers had been called to a "meeting" several miles away. They had not taken horses, and the thundering hooves in the ears of the villagers were more a sign of death than a sign of life.

Gunshots sounded as men ran out of their homes to inspect the disturbance. Horsemen threw firebrands onto roofs and into homes. Annie's hut filled with smoke.

"Come, *Pokni*!"

Annie pulled at her grandmother, who coughed uncontrollably.

"Keep low."

Annie propelled the old woman toward the door. Wiyot crawled outside and was instantly shot. Annie screamed and retreated into the house, choking on fumes and shock.

Moving to the back of the home, she began to furiously dig into the dirt floor. Between her frantic efforts and her small size, Annie managed to create a hole under the back wall large enough for her to escape. Once outside, she lay on her back, gasping, desperately trying to catch her breath so she could run.

The moonlight cast the shadow of a man over her. He looked down at her and made a *tsking* sound.

"Where are you going, gorgeous?"

He holstered his revolver and grinned. At that moment, Annie knew this man had worse things than bullets in store for her. She flipped to her stomach and scrambled to gain her footing. The man's heel caught her in the rump and sent her sprawling. He placed a boot squarely on her back. Moments later, an excruciating pain screamed through her shoulder.

Her attacker kneeled and showed her the cat-o'-nine-tails in his hand.

"Now," he hissed, "are you going to behave?"

Annie struggled, but his boot was still on her back. She could barely breathe.

"Yeehaw, boys, look what I got!"

The men didn't kill Annie. She was one of a few women and children who were "released" after the massacre. She was, however, alone. Where she found the strength to survive the rest of the war, or how she found peace, she did not know. Seeing the faces of some of the men who had assaulted her on body carts provided some finality to her ordeal, but instead of righteous satisfaction, she felt sadness. It seemed like the entire world was weeping. Annie longed for grace. And over the years, that longing developed into a desire to extend it, to the best of her ability, to everything and everyone she met.

Now, lying in bed, she blinked away the last of her tears and looked over at the man sleeping beside her. She knew his nightmares would come later.

CHAPTER FIVE

Again

THE CASE OF THE murders grew colder with the weather. Doyle was glad to see that Annie's anxiety had seemed to cool but noticed that she kept an eye on the road that passed by their claim, no doubt hoping for news from other homesteaders on their way to and from Weston.

Unfortunately, no one passed by, which was unusual, even considering the drop in temperature.

Doyle's nightmares became more regular and more unnerving. An owl joined him in his dreams, screeching at him and picking the faces of dead soldiers. Some nights, the bird transformed into a ghostly humanoid silhouette, tearing him apart as it screamed—always screamed—at him.

The double cruelty was that when the dreams ended, so did his sleep. As Doyle's insomnia progressed into the second week, he found himself irritable during the day and hallucinating, or at least overimagining things, in the dark. Almost every distant high-pitched sound was Ishkitini; every shadow was either a bloodthirsty killer or some vigilante who thought his "Indian" wife was somehow behind the deaths at the neighboring mining homestead.

One especially dark and early morning, after Doyle had thrashed, awoken, and retreated to the fireplace, Annie joined him.

"They are so bad, your dreams," she said softly, "so often, and so ..." She paused as though searching for the right word. "Evil."

The last word came out pointed, definite, and confident. It was the perfect description.

"They are frequent, yes, but nothing more," Doyle said, rubbing his weary eyes.

"I know they are more than that," Annie said. "You have not fought the sheets like this in years."

They sat in silence for a few moments, then Annie asked, "Is it because of the Stanley massacre?"

Doyle sighed. "I do not know where the dreams come from, Annie. I only know I need to sleep."

"You can seek healing before knowing the source, Doyle. Sometimes it has to be that way."

"The dreams will always be there," he said. "They will wax, and they will wane, but they will always be."

"Nothing will change unless you change it, Doyle." Annie's frustration was beginning to show. "You have not slept a full night in two weeks, and Harper mopes in his hut like a whipped dog. A long winter is coming, and all the provisions in the world will not sustain us if your heart fails."

With that, she walked quietly to the kitchen, placed three small potatoes into the pot, and set them over the fire. Doyle stared dully at the simmering pot. He wasn't yet sick of potatoes, but he was getting close. There was no sense in complaining. It was sustenance that would allow them to survive and, sometimes, survival was all one could hope for.

The following night, Doyle awoke again. It wasn't even a dream that woke him this time, and this intensely frustrated him. Would he ever sleep a full night again? His mind immediately filled with thoughts, worries, and tasks he needed to accomplish to ensure his family's safety through the winter. Annie stirred next to him.

"I am fine," he told her. "Go back to sleep."

Doyle left the bedroom to pace the floor. He was exhausted beyond measure. He was becoming a husk, losing his humanity—a humanity in which he didn't believe. There it was again. How could all men be evil if Annie was so good? If Harper was so loyal? Despite his best efforts, Doyle constantly found his thoughts returning to the paradox Annie had presented. It was still unresolved, continuing to churn as he lay awake each night.

Suddenly, he realized he was no longer comfortable with his belief. Perhaps that indicated there was indeed something of value within him worth holding on to. The goodness of mankind was too lofty an ideal. *And yet, there could be a glimmer, something worth investigating.* Almost immediately he remembered how he had just about lost his mind investigating "glimmers" when he first began searching for silver. Would he lose his mind looking for redemption too? What did it matter? Annie was right. He was already on the fast track to losing his sanity.

His thoughts flitted all over, again and again, all through the night. God in heaven, why couldn't he just shut it off?

Sitting at the table, he grabbed two fistfuls of hair in his hands and pulled for the simple relief of a single pain.

A shrill scream brought Doyle to his feet. His heart pounded. Had he fallen asleep again? It seemed real, but he couldn't be sure anymore. He looked through the bedroom doorway to see that Annie had bolted upright. Yes, this was real. She had heard it too. Doyle quickly crossed into the bedroom.

One look at Annie told him all he needed to know: Not a single owl seen or heard in seven years, then a murder, and now this ... demonic shriek in the middle of the night.

Doyle pulled on his pants.

"Doyle, no! Stay inside!"

"I just need to check."

He opened the front door, and Annie began to cry. He scanned the darkness outside but found nothing besides William, who looked up expectantly from his bed on the porch. Doyle abandoned his search and rejoined Annie in bed.

Words weren't necessary, and few passed between them that night. Doyle faced the reality that someone as evil as the life he had left was once again in his territory. And he knew Annie well enough to guess what she thought: demons long left behind had followed her here to again take what was most precious to her. Both had fled the wreckage of their previous lives to heal their scars in the desert, and both had been bitterly disappointed. And so, with nothing productive to do to ease their situation, they held each other that night, finding solace once again in their shared trauma.

CHAPTER SIX

Doyle's Resolution

THE FOLLOWING AFTERNOON, TWO men on horseback hailed Doyle and Harper while they ranged the herd. As they rode up to within speaking distance, Doyle could see that both men were armed and that they had been riding hard all day. Their chaps were well-dusted, and, despite the cold, a ring of sweat bled through their hat bands.

The first man, tall and clearly in charge, pulled his reins. "Afternoon."

Doyle and Harper nodded their greeting.

"Is one of you Mr. Doyle Hill?"

"I am," said Doyle cautiously, unnerved by the second unexpected visitation of strangers in as many weeks. "This is Rod Harper, my business partner. What brings you by?"

The visitors dismounted, and the ranchers followed suit.

"My name is Jacob Harris, and this is Andrew Thacker."

Thacker, shorter and seemingly a bit paranoid, touched his hat briefly before looking back out over the landscape.

"We have been dispatched to notify and warn homesteaders of Indian raids."

"We spoke to your wife a few weeks ago after the Stanley massacre," said Thacker.

"Has another ... attack occurred?" Harper asked.

"Yes," Harris replied, "last night."

Doyle immediately thought of the owl's shriek from the night before and felt his eyes widen.

Harper shifted his weight from one foot to the other. "Where?"

"Not far from here, but otherwise, it was the same as at the Stanleys. The whole family slaughtered in the night."

"Well, almost the whole family," Thacker said.

Annie rode up to the four men, bareback on her pony and a little out of breath.

"Afternoon, ma'am." Harris greeted her first.

Thacker nodded a curt greeting.

"You said 'almost the whole family.' There were survivors?" said Doyle to Thacker.

"Only one," he replied. "A ten-year-old girl."

Annie, apparently keen for details, cut in. "Did she see anything?"

Harris balked as though unsure he should say any more in Annie's presence.

"They found her in a crawlspace," Thacker said. "She claims to have seen the whole thing, but no one knows for sure."

Harris seemed to recognize that the cat was out of the bag. "The girl was in hysterics when the neighbor found her."

"What did she see?" Annie asked again.

"She said a monster killed her family," Harris said.

"A *monster*?" Harper repeated.

"Yes," Thacker piped up. "Pointy ears, claws. Huge. On two legs like a man, though—and feathers."

Harris gave Thacker an annoyed look, and everyone went silent. Doyle marveled at how closely the child's description aligned with what Annie had told him of the owl-witch many years ago: long, unnatural claws instead of fingers; long, pointed ears; a head taller than most men; and thick, ropey locks hanging from the head like bullwhips. It was enough to give anyone the chills, but to Annie, it was a known thing, devoid of mystery but full of terror.

For the first time, Doyle considered that there may be more to the realms of evil than he had fathomed. As far as he knew, the legend had originated with tribes that had never set foot in these parts. Annie would be the only local source of knowledge on the subject. And then there were the visiting owls. What man could send an owl to his home to scream fear into his wife? He didn't like to admit it, but there was something more to this than he could explain.

"Of course"—Harris broke the silence—"no one believes it. It is only in the mind of a hysterical child." He lowered his voice as if to provide Annie the option of not hearing his next words. "Chests ripped open, hundreds of stab wounds ... the carnage speaks for itself. It *has* to be Indians."

"I have seen Indian attacks," said Doyle. "They are not like this."

"Maybe Indians around here are different than what you are

used to," said Thacker, throwing a quick glance in Annie's direction.

This fool would not know an Indian if he was being scalped.

He stepped in front of Annie and leveled a glare at Thacker. "And what would you know about that?"

Doyle surprised himself. In one simple and natural reaction, he had placed himself between his wife and a potential threat. It was a minor act, but the fact that he hadn't had to force himself was an encouragement to him. Perhaps there was still some courage left in his heart.

Harper, fearless as always, drew himself up, hooked his thumbs into his belt, and sent a silent "say that again and see what happens" message.

Harris shot Thacker a sharp look.

"Enough, Andy." He then addressed the three homesteaders. "All we want to do is make sure you stay safe. And now, please excuse us. There are more families to warn, and it is getting late."

The next day, Doyle and Harper ranged their cattle a little farther than usual. The grass was beginning to go dormant, and they could not afford weak cattle going into the winter months, especially when their efforts were finally beginning to gather momentum.

Doyle was grateful for the opportunity to ponder. If nothing else, he entertained a small hope that he could think himself stupid enough for his mind to rest that night.

Annie rode flank, ostensibly to provide a third set of eyes, but really because she no longer cared to be alone. Doyle hadn't objected when she'd offered her assistance because he didn't want Annie to be alone.

His thoughts again wandered to the description of the murders. Whatever this thing was, it was purely evil. No animal slaughtered another save for utility, and there was no utility to be found here. There was no territory or young to be defended and no food sought. No man did this save one who had lost his mind or abandoned all reason in pursuit of desire. But what desire? To what end? No valuables appeared to be missing. Even livestock initially thought to be missing had been found wandering and quickly accounted for. A raving lunatic would surely have been found out by now, so Doyle dismissed that as a plausible explanation.

Doyle had never witnessed a single man commit such evil. During the war, both sides viewed support to the other side as treason and punished civilians severely for aiding or abetting the enemy. Punishments too often went from corrective or example setting and crossed the line into wanton violence. Men were often hanged in front of their families. Sometimes they were locked in their homes and burned alive. But it was always perpetuated by a group of men—men who banded together and forsook reason.

The surviving girl had described only one attacker; Doyle guessed this to be accurate. In a state of hysteria, he could imagine her seeing multiple monsters when only one existed, but for her to see only one when others were present seemed far less likely.

He was putting more effort into the thing than he liked. He hadn't moved across the country to solve a mystery. He had come to escape; to avoid evil, not to understand it. To abandon, as much as practical, society and self-seeking government, not to work together with them—regardless of the cause. Camber's words rose to his consciousness: "Has that worked for you?"

A thought struck him. What if he forced himself to face this fear? If he confronted this real-world evil, would he also defeat his nightmares and finally find peace? He was so tired.

What if I can solve this?

He tried to brush it all aside, but it was too late. The idea was growing inside him, and it now seemed reasonable—probable, even—that if he could find this killer, whatever it was, then he could restore peace to Annie and to himself.

At that moment, Doyle made up his mind. He would find whoever or whatever was responsible for this terror and kill it. He would do it alone; it would have to be alone. Enlisting anyone—even Harper—would diminish the redemption he sought. It was Harper who had rescued his yellow, fear-frozen hide from the battlefield nearly ten years ago at the cost of saving the wounded, crying Private Caskill. No. This time it was his turn. He, and he alone, would deliver Harper and Annie from harm. He alone would find out whether this thing was a demon or man, an unknown or known evil, a reason to believe in redemption or to, once and for all, reject any goodness in humankind.

"You all right there, boss?" Harper's voice shook him from his thoughts.

Doyle whirled around to see Harper. "Jeez, Rod! How long have you been back there?"

"Only just now. But you have not moved in ten minutes' time. Beginning to wonder if you were having a fit or finally getting some sleep."

"Where is Annie?"

Harper pointed to a solitary tree. Annie was taking full advantage of her pony's stature, grabbing bits of foliage and handing them to one of the calves as if it were her pet. She was too perfect. Had she been born a queen, the world would have half the trouble.

"How long are we staying, Hill?" Harper brought his attention back. He had dropped the patronizing "boss" and was now addressing him as a friend.

Doyle looked up at Harper to get a read. It had been a vague question, but the face told the rest. It was not the first time Harper had tried to have this discussion.

"Where would you have me go, Rod?"

"Texas."

"You would have us start over?"

Harper shrugged.

"This place is full of evil, and opportunities are much better there than here. You know this, Doyle. We are experienced cowboys. We will drive cattle and retire before the trains put us out of business."

Harper was right. They could make more in a few drives than they likely ever would raising cattle here to sell in Weston. It was the difference between thriving and surviving.

"And what of Annie? You would have her traveling the Chisholm with a band of strange men?"

Harper looked at Doyle in frustration. "We would only hire *good* men."

Doyle spat.

Good men. As if there is such a thing.

Yet here was Harper, loyal as ever. Did that not make him trustworthy?

"You remember Joe Grier's job offer right after the war? Driving cattle up the Chisholm Trail? San Antonio to Kansas City, Doyle. The man had money, and he liked you. By now, you would have been his trail boss."

Harper's voice held a note of hope, as though he thought this could be the time he finally convinced the Hills to strike this camp and head back to God's country. Doyle knew he had to end the conversation quickly. Partnering with Harper was one thing; partnering with a dozen more was out of the question. Men could not be trusted—especially in groups. Hunting this local killer was a big step; volunteering for the job that had nearly killed him would be another thing entirely.

"You should have stayed, Rod," Doyle said. "It was not my intention to waste you."

Doyle knew Harper didn't regret his decision. Although Harper's pride would never allow him to admit it, he was a lost sheep. After the war, with no real way to pay the debt he owed to Harper, Doyle had invited him to strike out West for gold. More loyal than adventurous, Harper had jumped at the chance, and the two had never separated.

Even if Harper depended on Doyle for emotional support—as Annie had suggested time and again—Doyle's greatest sense of obligation was to her. She depended on him emotionally *and* physically. She was his wife, and he her husband, and this was her home too. He had no desire to leave and would not uproot Annie unless she begged to quit the place.

"I will stay, Rod," Doyle said quietly. "You may stay or go. I will not think any less of you."

Harper chewed thoughtfully for a bit. "I may go."

Doyle examined his friend's face. This was unexpected. Harper was no bluff, so he must be weighing options. Was he growing independent? That would be a hard blessing for the Hills, but a blessing all the same. Harper felt no ties to the place, only to Doyle. Besides, now there was murder afoot. Perhaps the threat of the supernatural was pushing Harper to consider leaving. And why wouldn't it? Why stay when these atrocities robbed this place of its only redeeming quality?

"You know they will find it—him. They will find him and kill him."

"Even so," Harper replied, "maybe the demon is a sign."

There it was. Harper's comment validated Doyle's suspicion that the man's superstitious nature had been eating away at him. Another thing Harper would never admit. If Doyle had any remaining thoughts of including Harper on his quest, they now dissipated. Harper's notions could not be trusted any more than the vigilantes in town.

No. He would do this alone.

CHAPTER SEVEN

Hunting Ishkitini

In his dreams that night, Doyle stalked the bird in the darkness. Enraged by his courage, it retreated to a copse of trees, screaming and beating its wings at him. All at once, it was quiet.

Doyle made his way into the trees to see Ishkitini perched on the ground and staring at him. He stood taller than Doyle and was growing by the second. Without blinking, the demon shifted shape, wings giving way to lean gray arms. His bony elbows and knees jutted grotesquely as liquefying feathers dripped off his skin like hot tar. Claws slid from Ishkitini's hands. Doyle pointed his rifle and fired. Ishkitini lurched backward, regained his balance, and continued the metamorphosis as if nothing had happened. Doyle froze, lifeless, and considered himself dead. As if there all along, Harper was suddenly writhing underneath Ishkitini's talons, his head slowly being crushed.

"Hill! Do ... not ... leave ... me!"

Three clawed toes dug into Harper's chest; three more wrapped around his head and crushed his skull.

Something new caught the demon's eye. Doyle found his voice.

"Annie!"

She rushed toward Doyle. "Doyle! We need you ... I need you!"

The owl-witch turned his attention to her, and Doyle knew she would die. In the first act of heroism in any of his nightmares, he willed himself to action, pumping round after round into the creature's head in agonizing slow motion. Ishkitini screamed like a train engine, and Annie, shouting unintelligibly, pulled on his arm.

She was still pulling his arm when he awoke.

"He is here; Ofunlo shrieks," she screamed. The same owl he heard in his dreams, Annie had heard in the earthly plain. "There is another death."

If Doyle was honest, he wasn't so sure she was wrong.

The sound of William caught their ears. He was barking ... no, yelping! Something was out there with him.

Doyle grabbed his rifle and ran to the window.

"Doyle, *no!*"

Ranchers never backed down when their livestock was in danger, but right now, Annie wasn't a rancher; she was a wife.

"Doyle, please!"

William's hollering subsided, and Doyle hoped he had sent the intruder packing. He carefully opened the door and scanned the landscape.

"William!" he whispered.

No response. This wasn't good. If the dog was still on the chase, he'd be barking his head off. If not, he'd be back at the house. Harper's hut, too, was quiet.

That idiot, he thought. Doyle had half a mind to fire his gun to rouse him but held his resolve to investigate alone.

Doyle silently closed the door behind him and moved off the porch. He scanned the landscape for William, for the owl, anything. The cattle in the nearby corral were agitated but not under attack. His eyes rested on a scraggly grove of trees about fifty yards from the house. Something appeared to be moving, but he couldn't be sure.

"William!" Doyle called loudly.

In response, a shriek tore through the night, shaking Doyle's courage to the core. The movement in the trees stopped for a moment.

There is something there! He strained his eyes. It appeared to be standing—no, *growing*. Doyle's dream rushed back to him. Had it all been a premonition? The dark figure grew steadily before him, silhouetted against the moon-charged clouds. Again, Doyle found himself frozen. He could see the pointed ears and the oddly shaped head. Long, curved fingers hung from its arms.

Doyle was again paralyzed on the battlefield, and though Captain Feral's shouting voice fell silent on Doyle's ringing ears, the command on his lips was as clear as any bell.

Move!

Doyle dug deep inside himself.

"Move!" he hissed aloud.

Without warning, Doyle came alive again. He felt like he was watching himself from above as he charged forward in a run. He quickly closed the gap between the house and the grove, but the creature had a significant head start. Doyle crashed into the trees and saw what was left of William on the ground as he raced past. The dog's jaw was almost completely torn from his head, his limbs snapped and splayed grotesquely. Doyle felt instantly sick but shook it off. He was sure that if he stopped, he would be unable to move again.

He maintained his charge through the trees and toward a gully where the creature had disappeared. The scream came again, but Doyle was a man on fire. He would not stop until one of them was dead. Having no idea what it would take to bring this thing down, Doyle resisted the urge to fire into the darkness. He wanted every bullet to count.

As best he could manage in the dim moonlight, Doyle tracked the creature's movements along the creek bed as it moved in and out of sight, never providing a shot worth taking. Several minutes passed with no trace of the monster. Doyle, sure it had slipped away, began to mentally chart his course back home.

He caught sight of movement again, charged forward, then lost his quarry once more. Picking his way along the terrain a little at a time, Doyle paused every few steps to peer into the night and listen. He was the hunter now, yet the creature seemed to be toying with him. It didn't seem to be fleeing—in fact, at times, it almost appeared to be doubling back—but it was keeping its distance from Doyle. This was the game. Every time Doyle thought the demon had slipped away, he would catch sight again, and the chase would renew.

Finally, after a frustrating twenty minutes with no sign of his quarry, Doyle concluded that he'd lost the trail. He needed to get back to the house. Annie was likely beside herself, and he needed to check on Harper as well. Once that was done, he would then find a way to dispose of William before Annie found him.

Doyle gave one last look to ensure he was alone, then turned toward the house. A screech erupted in his ear, knocking him off-balance. He fell backward into the creek bed, his head connecting with the rocks beneath him as thrashing wings beat the air around him.

And everything went dark and quiet once again.

"Doyle! Doyle!"

It was nearly daybreak when Annie's frantic voice finally roused Doyle.

"Doyle, what happened?"

Harper was there too, gently moving Doyle into a sitting position. From the moment his eyes fluttered, Harper peppered him with questions.

"What were you doing out here?"

"What did you see?"

Annie began to choke up. "Oh, Doyle, you fool man! Are you hurt?"

Hill held up his hand in silent protest.

"Okay, okay, just rest," Annie said.

"There is no sign of foul play," Harper observed. "He must have lost his way in the dark and fallen."

Doyle slowly got to his feet, waving Harper away when he moved to support him.

Harper wandered down the riverbank. "I will keep looking for anything suspicious," he called.

Annie began to ease her husband back to the house. "You will need to see a doctor."

"No doctor," Doyle replied. "I just need to get rid of this headache."

"You are lucky to still have a head." Annie spat.

She shifted uncomfortably under the weight of Doyle's right arm. "What were you thinking running after ... after ... oh, what did you see?"

"It was only a man," he lied. Annie would have believed the truth, of course; Doyle had no doubts about that. What he doubted was her ability to handle it. Doyle trusted his wife yet didn't trust her.

Annie, however, was clearly more angry than fearful. "You will not leave the house today," she ordered, "and I am sending Harper for a doctor as soon as he gets back."

"No. No doctor."

"Yes."

"I will stay here today, but I will not see a doctor. I am fine."

"Suit yourself," Annie relented, and Doyle, too weak to argue about anything but the doctor's visit, reluctantly accepted his punishment.

Later that morning, Harper's standard knock came at the cabin door. Annie let him in, then immediately returned to Doyle's side.

From his position on the bed, Doyle could see Harper moping in the main room, and it annoyed him. He didn't need another wife to fret over him. Presently, Annie left the room to brew a tea, and Harper carefully approached the bedroom to seek a private audience with Doyle. Harper was not a complete ruffian, and being in any woman's bedroom was uncomfortable, if not improper.

"Annie said there was an owl screeching last night, and you went looking for the Ishkitini."

Doyle pretended to scoff.

"What did you see out there, Hill?"

The directness of Harper's question caught Doyle off guard. He hadn't yet processed the events of the night. He knew two things: First, there was something out there that Doyle couldn't account for. Not human, not animal. Second, he had proven himself a little last night, and it felt like an accomplishment. He needed to see this through on his own.

"Who says there was anything besides an owl?"

Harper looked betrayed. "I found the dog."

"William." Doyle silently remembered his plans to hide the dog's remains.

Harper put up his hand. "I hid him, Doyle." He jerked his head toward the kitchen. "No sense in her seeing that right now. Especially considering the fit she was in when she pulled me out of bed."

Harper's sullenness now made sense. He was worried. And yet he had put that aside to protect Annie when Doyle couldn't, and for that, Doyle was more than grateful. He was proud. Perhaps Harper was stronger than Doyle gave him credit for. Was this man not worthy of his trust? Was he not courageous enough to bear the truth? Perhaps. But it wasn't simply about trusting Harper or even protecting Annie. It was also about proving himself courageous—if only to himself. Excluding others still seemed right to him, even if he didn't understand it.

No. He would see this through on his own.

Doyle studied Harper's face for a moment as he let the decision sink in. "There is something out there, Rod. I do not know what."

CHAPTER EIGHT

Town Hall

FOUR DAYS LATER, RIDERS once again visited the homestead. It was late morning when Jacob Harris rode up to the yard. Doyle noticed that John Baker, the storekeeper, now accompanied Harris instead of Thacker.

Doyle held his breath as he and Harper joined Annie in the yard. Gone were the days when unexpected visits merely made him suspicious. Visitors only brought bad news now.

He looked up at Baker and Harris. "Another?"

Harris nodded and dismounted. Baker followed suit.

"Who was it this time?" Harper asked, beating Annie to the punch.

"The homestead just past the Suttons'," Baker said. "Not that far from you."

"How many?" Doyle asked.

"Two. A woman and ... and a baby."

Annie gasped. "Nooo." She looked sick.

Everyone fell quiet.

"They still think it is Indians?" Harper asked.

"That is the prevailing theory, yes," Harris acknowledged, "but …"

Doyle looked up quickly. *He knows something!* "But what?"

Annie turned and slowly began to walk back to the house.

"Well …" Baker began, "some of us doubt that theory, but we are in the minority."

"Why is that?" Harper asked.

Baker furrowed his brow. "Because last night's attack was stealthy. There was no yelping and howling, no riding in on horses. A single horse went missing around dusk—either got out or was let out, no one knows. The murders happened when the rest of the family was searching for the animal."

Harris's horse nipped at Baker's, and Harris pulled the reins in retaliation. "I suppose it could still be Indians, but it does not seem likely to me."

Doyle sighed. He wondered if he would see the killer again or if he had chased it off his property for good. Had it moved on? Part of him wanted it to be true, but there was a part of him—a growing part—that needed to face the thing once more.

The unruly horse leaned into the other, and Harris yanked the reins impatiently. "There is more to discuss," he told Doyle. "In addition to notifying the public, the sheriff has also reported the killings to the army outpost. There is also a town hall tomorrow afternoon. The mayor will announce a reward for the capture or killing of the murderers and tell everyone if army protection can be provided."

Harper looked at Doyle, an expectant expression on his face. Two weeks ago, Doyle would have rejected the invitation outright. Now, however, he wanted to find out what others thought. He was also intensely curious to discover what others *knew*. Had anyone seen what he had seen? Attending the town hall may be the only opportunity to find out.

"We will be there."

The next morning, Doyle and Harper headed into town with Annie, leaving their little herd corralled. So far, the demon had hunted only at night, but Doyle was taking no chances, going as far as to concoct reasons for Annie and Harper to join him, in the event they wanted to stay behind. His life was made easier when they both announced their intent to go.

Doyle found the meeting to be even more unpleasant than he had imagined. Although the meeting had been limited to men over the age of sixteen, there were more than enough homesteaders and townspeople to pack the stuffy courthouse with men and opinions until the air hung thick with body odor, vengeance, and rash assumptions.

"The Indian tribes are trying to scare us into abandoning our claims," said a small, wiry man.

"They have declared war on the railroad," said another. "They are trying to fulfill the pagan prophecy from their gods."

To the warmongers in the meeting, it seemed that only a motive had to be agreed upon in order to establish the guilt of the indigenous people. Most of the townsfolk had been spared the worst of the war and, therefore, the worst of humanity. Indian reprisal was familiar, and as such, the facts were pressed into the mold of their theory.

Doyle and Harper exchanged a few glances when the details of the murders clearly pointed to a single killer or when descriptions of the scenes matched the state in which the men had found William's body. Otherwise, the two men sat silently, letting the speculations swirl in the air like confetti.

Most of the army posts within a hundred miles had been either drawn down or abandoned at the end of the war. Several others were still supporting security operations after protracted skirmishes with the Native American tribes further west. Help would come, but it would take time.

And, so, no closer to any helpful solution, the meeting ended.

If the ominous weather had been a predictor of the night's events, then the storm that unleashed during the meeting would have been a bad sign indeed. By the time things adjourned, it was evident no one was going anywhere until the rain moved on. It was unseasonal, which made the mood in town even more eerie. Weather aside, Doyle was not interested in trying to make it back once dusk came. The cattle herd would be fine in the elements, but he would not entrust Harper and Annie to the night. Most other homesteaders who had made the trip into Weston likely felt the same and began arranging board in town for the night.

John Baker repaid Doyle and Harper's offer of assistance after the first murder by providing the Hills with a room above his store. Harper, as Doyle expected, refused to join them, opting instead for a blanket and the stable behind the storefront.

Although his sleep had improved over the past week, Doyle found himself lying awake once more. Truthfully, he would have felt safer here than out on the plain had it not been for the mob mentality during the afternoon's proceedings. Doyle was sure that after the meeting had concluded and he met back up with Annie, he had seen Andy Thacker, Jacob Harris's first rider dispatch companion, eyeing her suspiciously. The whole thing made Doyle uncomfortable.

Doyle slipped out of bed and over to the little window where he could look down into the street. The storm had passed, leaving behind a soft rain. He noticed the lights in the saloon and began to wonder what the mood was like inside. Were the patrons riling themselves up? Were they telling ghost stories, passing fiction back and forth as fact until they found a scapegoat? Did anyone else know the killer wasn't human?

How he wished for a way to dispel the myths that only served to obstruct justice. But he'd seen people in this state before. Momentum was gathering, and everyone had theories. Even if he was willing to share what he'd seen, he felt it would make no difference now.

He looked at Annie. She was safe enough here, and if she woke to a note, she wouldn't be too worried to find he'd slipped out. He'd write a quick message to Annie, then check on Harper and see if he wanted a drink.

Doyle made his way downstairs and outside to the stable, where he found Harper asleep among the smell of damp alfalfa and farm animals. Deciding it wouldn't be worth the effort it would take to wake him, Doyle made his way across the muddy street alone. He would pop into the saloon, grab a drink, gauge the public temperament, and then try to get some rest.

As unobtrusively as possible, Doyle made his way inside and to the bar.

A potbellied, mustached man with round glasses approached Doyle. Several spoons and a rag peeked above the pocket of his barman's apron. "What will it be?"

"A whiskey. Thank you."

Doyle nursed the glass in his hand as he drank in everything his ears could capture. The general mood, while not jovial, was not as serious as he had expected. Instead of the rabble-rousing he had feared, the conversations seemed to center more around the deceased, their families, and what people knew of them. It surprised him. He was not so naive as to think there was no malicious talk, but what he heard—or rather did not hear—put him at greater ease. People seemed to feel safe enough in each other's company, and whether he admitted it or not, Doyle envied them. They so easily seemed to have cast off their cares after the afternoon's unpleasantness.

A scream echoed through the gaslit streets. Doyle and four others burst through the door to find a working girl lying in the flooded ditch outside the saloon. Blood soaked her clothes faster than the now-driving rain could rinse off. She clutched her throat. Doyle had seen this type of wound before. She was cut badly, and he doubted she would last more than a few minutes. He turned his attention to the streets and searched for her assailant.

A distant streetlamp threw a shadow over a single figure as it ducked into an alley. Without thinking, Doyle bolted after it. He had to see Ishkitini again; he had to understand what it was.

Sprinting across the street, he barreled around the side of the building and dashed down the alley, ignoring the shouts of the men running after him. He had to get there first, *he* had to put the kill shot through the demon's heart. Everyone else could get in line—or finish the job if Doyle failed.

The back of the alley teed into another building and Doyle had a decision to make. Right or left. He stopped and listened, taking the opportunity to pull his Colt from his clothes since, according to the custom of polite civilization, he hadn't strapped the holster to his side that day.

The other pursuers would be closing in on him soon—he had to decide, now!

A movement caught his eye to the left, and Doyle, gun in hand, ran left. That alley dead-ended, closed in on all sides by two-story structures. Ishkitini would have to fly if he wanted to escape this time. Doyle had him boxed in.

From behind stacked crates, a low growl warned Doyle to keep his distance. He pulled up short and leveled his pistol at the crates. Carefully, finger on the trigger, he sidestepped around the stack.

His pressure on the trigger increased. The slightest start would mean a bullet in the monster. Still, Doyle wanted the shot to count. Taking one final deep breath, Doyle stepped into the plain view of a street mutt, snarling and growling at the man who had chased and cornered him in a back alley.

Cursing aloud, Doyle backed a safe distance away from the dog, then dejectedly walked back toward the saloon. One of the men joined him.

"You let him get away? Why did you not shoot?"

"It was only a mutt," Doyle said. "I chased the wrong shadow."

They returned to the scene of the crime to find that the woman had died and that panic was building among those gathered around. The killers of the plains were now here—in town—where everyone thought themselves safe. Sheriff Schutz and several others continued the hunt, quickly spreading out to canvass all of Weston. Almost immediately, the people in the street began to speak of monsters and Indians. Doyle recognized, without satisfaction, that this was the kind of talk he had expected when he went inside the saloon.

"Him! Right there!"

A man was pointing at him. It was Thacker. The small crowd turned their attention from the man to Doyle. Doyle moved closer to the group to show he had nothing to hide.

"What about me?" he asked.

The man continued to speak as if Doyle wasn't there.

"We got settlers being killed out there, one of our own killed under our noses! This railroader shows up with that—that savage woman, and now we—"

Doyle exploded over the rest of his sentence, pinning him against the saloon's outside wall. He grabbed a fistful of the man's hair and jerked it backward, exposing his neck. Doyle had drawn his knife.

The man, frozen in surprise, didn't move.

"You have not *seen* savage!" he roared.

He wanted to cut Thacker's throat right there, but thankfully, he was not as rash as some. Doyle instead leaned into the man's ear and hissed, "If you so much as look at my wife again, *everyone* will know exactly what *savage* looks like!"

They stood there for what seemed like an hour, breathing heavily. The shocked onlookers stood motionless.

He knew the touch on his arm without looking. Without a word, Annie pushed the knife away from Thacker and replaced the hair in Doyle's hand with her own fingers. Doyle knew he'd reacted badly, but if his actions had confirmed the townspeople's bias, Annie's gentle response did so much more. She undid Doyle's tantrum, nullified Thacker's words, and softened the prejudice of those willing to challenge their assumptions.

Doyle couldn't decide whether he should offer an apology or simply slink away. Thacker was caught between gratefulness and the humiliation of being saved by the woman he'd insulted. Everyone else had been given something unexpected to consider. Harper, who had arrived with Annie, appeared to be just as uncomfortable as Doyle. Annie, however, was serene—to the point of seeming oblivious to the unpleasantness swirling around her.

A commotion about forty yards up the main street quickly dissipated the awkward scene.

"Git off me, you sons of ... *Aah*! Lemme go!"

Kicking and swearing, a man was dragged from the shadows by deputies, and several men, including Baker, rushed over to assist.

Word quickly spread that the sheriff's men had found the murderer between buildings, trying to shed his bloody clothes.

John returned and escorted the Hills and Harper back to their accommodations to ensure no one bothered them. Doyle stopped by the rear entry door to the building while Annie made her way up the stairs.

"Thank you again for allowing us to stay. We will be on our way as soon as we settle accounts tomorrow."

"You settle accounts as you see fit, Doyle, but I consider them even. I just want to make sure you are all safe." John turned to Harper. "Are you sure you will not sleep in the building?"

Harper shrugged. "Mr. Baker, I am not convinced that I am any safer here than in the open country."

John seemed to consider this for a moment. "He confessed as soon as they hauled him into the station, you know."

Doyle scoffed. "He was drenched in her blood. What was there left to confess?"

"The girl spurned the killer's ... insufficient fare earlier this week. He nursed a grudge until he had the opportunity to cut her throat. He thought everyone would just think the Indians struck again."

Harper shook his head disgustedly. "Next thing you know, they will be raving about the railroad, how it is bringing criminals into town. Is there no end to the blame?"

John scowled. "It is all the same, I suppose. Evil begets evil, and this whole thing is making fools of us all."

Harper and the Hills returned home the next day to find that their herd had found its way out of the corral and wandered. It was, after all, nothing more than a circular fence. It took most of that day to recover them.

All was quiet over the next few days. Annie still had a sadness about her, and Harper barely spoke a word. Doyle was moody. The short-lived comfort of the company of the saloon's patrons was all too quickly replaced with resentment for the community. There was no deliverance except in killing the demon. If he was to be hunted one way or another—either by the supernatural or by his own kind—he would take his chances on the desert plain over that court of fools in town. They could not be trusted, and the best he could do was to rely on his own sense of right.

Has that worked for you?

Camber's challenge had been a rock in Doyle's shoe for weeks, yet Doyle still felt his answer hadn't changed. Well enough, not perfect, but better than anything else he could think of.

CHAPTER NINE

The Last

FOR NOW, THE NIGHTS were quiet. Annie worried daily that the owl would return; Doyle expected it.

In fact, he waited for it each night. He wondered if the demon himself shrieked or somehow bid the owls to call on his behalf. Then, just as quickly, he would marvel that he was even asking such questions. The very idea had seemed preposterous to him only a month ago, and yet here he was trying to figure out if a demon was wielding control over birds.

Doyle took to sleeping at the threshold of the cabin in hopes he could catch the thing off guard. This also seemed silly. How was he supposed to get the drop on the devil? He was eager for another encounter. He needed to end this, to find redemption, to know the truth, to find peace. He needed to *sleep*!

Each uneventful night prompted his mind to again build nightmares around his anxieties. Each night he hunted Ishkitini. Sometimes he engaged in hand-to-hand combat, desperately trying to grip the demon's soft, putrid flesh while oozing, sopping feathers coated his hands like oil. Sometimes Harper and Annie stood a short distance off, staring as if in a trance. Other times Doyle emptied his Henry into the monster in the middle of the town square while everyone else went about their business. It comforted him to know that, although he never killed the beast in his dreams, he was finally taking action—a welcome change from the war dreams in which he lay frozen in terror and shame.

"Doyle," Annie said as her husband prepared to spend another night at the threshold of the cabin. "You are a greater comfort to me in bed."

"I cannot let him get the jump on us," he replied.

"Doyle, you cannot destroy him with lead! Spend what time we have together with me."

Doyle looked into her pleading eyes. "Annie, I will protect you first, then I will comfort you. Let me end this."

He would not be moved. He was convinced something was coming for them.

Annie put her hand on Doyle's face and looked into his eyes. "What are you not telling me?"

Doyle rubbed his face with his palms and said nothing.

That night, in his dreamscape, as the cattle grazed lazily in the distance, he pinned the mortally wounded Ishkitini to the ground and, with knife in hand, prepared to cut the scream out of his throat. Ishkitini glared at him in hateful defiance, filled his bleeding lungs, and howled deafeningly, knocking him out of his own dream.

Doyle lay still, panting on the floor, unsure if the sound was real or not. This dream felt different. He felt that this time, had he not woken, one of them would have died.

He listened for Annie but heard nothing. She was still asleep, so it was likely only in his dreams—dreams, dreams, dreams! Dreams in which he never saw the creature die; dreams which ended right before he fully prevailed. True, he had never died either, but something had shifted.

A creak on the porch yanked him from his thoughts. It couldn't have been more than six feet from his head. Doyle jumped up and fairly ripped the door from the hinges. A sudden noise in the bedroom told him that Annie, too, was awake now.

"Doyle, *no! Please!*"

Doyle posted himself in the doorframe, rifle shouldered. "Stay put, Annie! Take the Colt on the table!"

Seeing movement outside the cabin, Doyle followed his rifle out the door. The demon growled threateningly as it stole around the side of the house.

Suddenly, out of nowhere, the preacher's words hit him again.

Has that worked for you?

It *had* worked, but it didn't work anymore. Doyle felt overwhelmingly alone.

What am I doing?! he thought. He was human, and humans could only survive in community. Why was he abandoning his pack for a solo hunt?

"Harper!" Without a second thought, Doyle fired two rounds to wake Harper. "Harper, I need you! Help me!"

Knowing reinforcements were on the way, Doyle bolstered his

courage and rounded the corner of the house as quickly as he dared—just in time to see the monster making for the boulders to the south. It wasn't a clean shot by any stretch but Doyle had to take it. He was committed. He vowed that by the end of the night, he would be either fully dead or fully alive. Even if he missed, it would awaken the groggy Harper, who could protect Annie should any harm befall Doyle.

He brought the rifle to his shoulder and cracked off the best shot he could manage. To his astonishment, the monster yelped as it dove behind the rocks.

Throwing too much caution aside, Doyle charged around the boulders and felt the claws rip through the flesh of his face, knocking him to the ground. Hot blood ran into his eyes, obscuring his vision. Desperate, he swung and grappled with one arm and reached for his rifle with the other. He had shot it, had he not? Was the monster immune to lead?

His hand scrambled along the ground for the rifle. It was no good. The Henry had been thrown too far to be recovered now. The long talons fell hard and fast, tearing Doyle to ribbons. In a last offensive, he grabbed the creature's head, afraid that once the beak opened, his face would be torn off. The head began to give way, coming apart in Doyle's hands and peeling away from the body like the feathers in his dreams.

Ishkitini shrieked in rage. His claws, hard and cold, punctured the skin of Doyle's throat, pinning him to the ground. Any movement would drive them deeper and surely kill him.

Ishkitini's molting head fell to the ground, but the creature's strength remained. The only blood was Doyle's. And in this moment, it dawned on Doyle that the demon had lured him in with a false cry of pain.

What evil is this? The demon leaned over him, hot breath puffing fog into the freezing air. Doyle blinked hard to clear the blood from his eyes and gasped, his voice of utter betrayal scarcely a croak under the blades on his throat.

"Har ... Harper?"

A knee sank into Doyle's chest, and he coughed, struggling for breath under the weight of it.

"Harper! What are you *doing*?" Doyle gasped.

Ishkitini leaned over him.

"Why are you hunting me alone in the night?" Doyle's brain reeled. "Why? What ... is this?"

Harper's eyes were different: cruel and more alive somehow. It was as if he'd played a dullard his whole life only to reveal himself in this moment.

"Did you think, Doyle, that you are the only one who does not sleep?" he asked.

The question was rhetorical, and Doyle did not answer.

"You should never have endeavored to end this on your own!" Harper hissed reproachfully. "Now it is *your* end, *your* undoing!"

It still didn't make sense.

"Did you kill them?"

Harper stared coldly in silent answer.

"Children? Mothers?"

Silence.

A helpless rage began to grow under Doyle's shock. All the wrong he had tried to escape, all the right he had tried to live, the evil he wanted to forget. Now here it was in a form he never would have fathomed.

"What ... possesses you, Harper?" He despaired.

"It is only myself," Harper replied. "Nothing more."

That was it. Harper had no grand design, no master plan. He had no explanation for his actions and did not pretend otherwise. Doyle's head swam as he felt for his Colt, momentarily forgetting that he'd left it with Annie a lifetime ago in the house a million miles away. He was already in a different dimension—he was a dead man.

Doyle tried to move beneath the claws on his throat. "I cannot understand."

"It does not do to dwell, Doyle. It cannot be understood. This seems good to me, and I will do as I see fit." He paused for a moment, as though unsure how to finish. "... until ... until I cease to be."

Harper drove the claw-spikes he had fashioned deep into Doyle's throat, delivering the last violence he would ever see. Almost immediately, Doyle began to fade. He could hear Annie calling for him in the distance. Panic surged in him, and he stared intensely into Harper's eyes.

"Do not worry ..." Harper spoke to him again, his voice muffled and warped by Doyle's slowing brain waves. "... I will ... no one will suspect her."

Doyle's vision left. He blinked hard and the darkness enveloped him.

And somewhere above, the owl screamed.

PART II
DESCENT INTO MADNESS

EVERYONE HAS TURNED AWAY, ALL HAVE BECOME CORRUPT;
THERE IS NO ONE WHO DOES GOOD, NOT EVEN ONE.
PSALM 53:3

THE HEART IS DECEITFUL ABOVE ALL THINGS AND BEYOND CURE.
WHO CAN UNDERSTAND IT?
JEREMIAH 17:9

CHAPTER TEN

Not a Man

Indian Territory
Spring 1863

Harper exhaled slowly, gently squeezing the trigger of his rifle. He'd done this at least a thousand times, but it didn't matter. The gunshot always startled him.

The gun bucked hard into his shoulder, and his eyes slammed shut. He opened them to see both horse and rider disappearing the way they had come. He cursed aloud. It had been a long shot, sure, but that made no difference to him. In his mind he'd failed, misjudged the wind, led the target too much, winced like a coward when the gun went off. In any case, he'd failed. Instead of a clean kill, a complete miss. Instead of victory, failure. Instead of disappearing, the Yankee scout would report another rebel position.

Sergeant Johnson crashed into Harper's position and grabbed him roughly by the shoulder. "What are you playing at, boy?"

Harper opened his mouth to reply, but it made no difference. The sergeant had already manufactured Harper's response and deemed it unacceptable.

He cuffed Harper hard on the back of the head. "Answer me when I speak to you!"

Harper spoke quickly to avoid another blow. "Sergeant, it was a scout. He—"

"Liar!" came the automatic rebuttal.

It was always the same reaction, devoid of logic. No matter what Harper said, it was always a lie. The sergeant shoved him to the ground. Johnson was ill-tempered at best, and his weariness brought out his worst; moreover, he hated Harper. He never had a logical reason for this, so, like most people, he wove a blanket of assumptions in which his prejudice could comfortably rest. Harper was a moron, a glory seeker, and his ineptitude was a constant threat to the safety of others.

By now, the rest of the patrol had responded to the gunshot and gathered around the commotion.

"You cannot tell a Yankee from your mother! How would you even know what to shoot? Or, in this case, what to miss?"

The men chuckled.

"He was wearing blues," Harper said.

Johnson reached down for Harper's rifle. Expecting to be struck again, Harper cringed and was instantly filled with self-hatred. Who cringes but a guilty man? Who expects abuse but one deserving it? Harper was a fool; he had put the patrol in danger, had no business in the company of men, and deserved to be beaten.

In a flash, Johnson was on top of him, the blows falling swiftly and painfully. Knowing better than to resist, Harper simply tried to block Johnson's fists until the smaller, senior man wore himself out.

Puffing, Sergeant Johnson snatched Harper's rifle from the ground and pulled himself upright. "You ..." He caught his breath. "... are *not* a *soldier*." He gestured toward the others. "You are not worthy to carry my soldiers off a battlefield. Your job is to save my men, not pilfer the weapons of those you allow to die!" He shook the rifle in the air. "This belongs to *soldiers!* So help me, God, I will shoot you with the next gun I see you touch."

The company dispersed, leaving Harper to smolder in Johnson's reproach. He half wished Johnson had destroyed him with lead instead of words. He wouldn't admit it, but he believed every bit of it. As soon as he had missed the shot, he'd remembered immediately why he had no business in the company of men, that he was worthless, and that he brought misfortune to everyone around him. Even so, it was hard to hear it from another, harder still to have everyone else hear it too.

The deep brutality of the matter was that Johnson was wrong, Harper was wrong, and every man there who said nothing was wrong. Every bit of it was a lie.

Early Spring 1860

Rodney Harper was fourteen years old and a good-sized boy for his age. He sat in the dark, gritting his teeth and swallowing hard at the lump that persisted in his throat. He worked his shirttail across the split skin over his eye. Through the heat of anger, he could feel the dull ache of his broken nose and the tight skin around his swollen face. He sweated continuously in the warm evening air and tried to control his breathing. Rage, shame, fear, and despair swirled inside him to the point that he could hardly think.

He lay on his back in the little barn and sighed shakily as he began to recount the events of the day.

"Rod, girls, I want you to meet someone," his mother had said.

She stood before the children with a younger man whom Rod recognized as their distant neighbor. She seemed awkwardly excited.

"You all know Mr. Jass ..." She paused, clearly not having adequately prepared for the conversation.

Mr. Jass reached down and boldly grabbed her hand.

"Mr. Jass, I mean Stuart, well, we are married," she said. "He is going to be your new father."

"What?" Rodney exploded. "This is what you were doing at church?"

Her countenance became stern. "Rod!"

Wincing at the painful memory, Rod shifted on the barn floor. His mother always called him Rod these days. When he was young, it was "little Rodney," then Rodney, and finally just Rod. It made sense, these transitions. Rod was the oldest, the only boy, and, since the passing of his father, he had been the workhorse of his family's subsistence farm. He had matured by necessity so that by the age of fourteen, he looked and acted more like a man than a child.

Unfortunately, everyone around him, including his mother and now Mr. Jass, expected him to reason like a man.

"Mama, how could you?" Rod said, shameful tears filling his eyes.

"Enough," Mr. Jass said abruptly.

Rod looked from Mr. Jass to his mother.

"Look here, son, look at me."

Rod turned his gaze on his new stepfather.

"I am here because your mother cannot run this farm on her own. I know a thing or two about such matters and so we, as a family"—his eyes widened at these words for emphasis—"are going to turn it around so that we may survive."

Rod ignored him. "Mama, I was running the farm, I was doing everything Papa taught me. We were doing fine!"

Rod's sisters' wide eyes went from him to their mother to their stepfather. Four-year-old Jill, the youngest, began to whimper, and nine-year-old Kate instinctively put her arms around the younger girl.

"Rod, you are not a man," said the new Mrs. Jass. "We need a man to ensure our survival."

Rod was insulted. What had he done besides what his father had taught him? "But I am a man!"

"Enough!" Mr. Jass repeated. "I am your father now, and you are my son."

Emboldened, Rod's mother stepped forward and addressed her offspring. "Children, obey your parents."

Rod's middle sister, seven-year-old Millie, took a tentative step toward Mr. Jass, who dropped to one knee.

“Yes, that’s it!” he encouraged. “Come here, little one.”

Jass opened his arms and folded her into them. In seconds, the other two girls ran to him. Rod stood in disbelief, feeling as though his entire family had been duped.

“He is not my father!” Rod shouted.

Mr. Jass stood up. “Rodney, come with me.”

Rod looked once again to his mother. “Mama, I—”

“Obey your father,” she said, although visibly less sure of herself than she was two minutes ago.

Rod gave one last entreating look at his mother, then looked at Jass, who jerked his head toward the door. With no one to defend him against this injustice, Rod hung his head and followed his stepfather out of the house, across the overly large yard, and to the barn. Here in Texas, land was plentiful, and in the decades preceding Rod’s birth, his family had been one of the thousands of land-grabbers that flooded the area in search of a better future.

Mr. Jass opened the door to the barn and ushered Rod inside.

He better not think he is about to whip me.

Rod had barely crossed the threshold of the barn when the man grabbed his shirt collar and threw him to the ground. He went sprawling. By the time he had flipped onto his back, Mr. Jass had grabbed him again. He threw Rod into the wall, stunning him. Jass’s hair fell into his eyes so that he looked crazed.

“I have not met a horse I cannot break, and you best believe I will break you,” he said. “There will be one man in this household, do you understand?”

Rod saw red and jumped to his feet.

"It is my home! What have you done to earn it besides courting my mother?"

"Wrong answer, boy," Jass muttered.

He swung his fist, and Rod's nose exploded in blood. He grabbed his face in shock.

Jass had gone over the edge. He caught Rod in the eye, then the chin, pummeling his face with the fervor of a bare-knuckle boxer.

"Spare the Rod, spoil the child—is that not the family joke?" He threw his stepson to the ground once more. "You have run your family's farm into the ground, and I am here to pick up what's left. You will not cross me again." Jass spat on the ground and rubbed his knuckles. "I do not want to see you back in my house." He turned and left Rod covered in his own blood.

CHAPTER ELEVEN

Leaving Home

Rod had distanced himself from the house until dark, letting himself into the barn once he knew everyone was asleep. It was unclear whether Stuart's intention was to kick him out of the house or off the property, for a night, a few days, or forever.

Rod did not want to stay but had nowhere to go. He had nothing on him besides clothing, and he would not make it far without anything to sustain himself. He did not know if Stuart would eventually let him back in the home again to retrieve his belongings, but he didn't want to ask only to be beaten off the property—*his* property.

Well, *Stuart's* property. The thought that his farm now belonged to Stuart angered him beyond measure. His thoughts unexpectedly turned to the possibility of killing Stuart. The idea of vengeance felt good. Besides, if he did murder Stuart, he would only be protecting his own person and property. His mother had made a poor choice; perhaps she deserved to lose another husband.

He fantasized about spilling Stuart's blood but recognized that he would have to be crafty. Everything would have to be carefully orchestrated so that he would not come under suspicion. Rod wanted to be the last thing that Stuart saw, to watch the man's eyes as they became lifeless.

The idea that no one, even Stuart, could know that it was Rod who killed him was so unsatisfying that he completely forgot about vengeance and turned his attention to leaving his old life behind. Rod accepted that he was dishonorable, but he felt his least dishonorable option now was to leave.

Once his mind was made up, he moved quickly. He was a coward—he hadn't even fought back against his stepfather—and any delayed action would result in paralysis. He scoured the barn for anything of value, reminding himself that he was not stealing; everything here belonged to him. He quietly saddled his nag and stuffed what excess tackle and tools he could into a feed sack. Not daring to burglarize his home for anything else, he quietly led the horse to the edge of his property before mounting and heading toward town. He couldn't stay there, but perhaps he could wait until morning and trade some of his property for food. After that, he'd decide where to go next.

Rod figured he had at least four hours past daybreak to buy what he could and get out of town before Stuart noticed the missing horse and came after him. Even so, there was no guarantee that Stuart would not pursue him beyond the town. His mother would not come for him, but Stuart would come for his horse.

Rod loitered for hours at the little outpost until it finally came to life. At the first sign of activity around the store, he hitched his horse and went inside.

"Young Harper." The clerk, Mr. Ames, greeted him. "What brings you in s—"

He broke off, staring at Rod's swollen face.

"Good morning, Mr. Ames," Harper said, silently annoyed at the patronizing "Young Harper" moniker. He was pretty sure he knew what Ames thought of him. He was the fool boy who had run his family's farm into the dirt. The boy whose mother had to sell out to a hack like Stuart Jass just to survive. The butt of everyone's jokes.

"I need to trade some things."

Ames raised an eyebrow but said nothing about Rod's appearance. "What do you have?"

"Just some old tackle and a few tools. Everything is in working order."

"And why are you off-loading them?" Ames asked.

"They are surplus. And we have need of supplies for a trip that Mr. Ja ... my new stepfather is taking."

Rod knew he had to play it cool or risk raising shrewd Mr. Ames's suspicions.

Convince him the Harper-Jass clan is a happy family, then be on your way.

"Where is he going?"

"I am not sure. One of the cities with a lot of ranches."

Ames chuckled. "Oh, well, that'd be either way up north or way down south," he said. "Roughly the same provisions either way. Who all is going?"

Rod didn't like the way Ames chuckled at him like he was an idiot boy who should already know where the largest Texas ranches were located.

"Just him. How long does it take to get to those places?"

"Oh, I do not know ... three, four days. What is he looking for there that he cannot get here?"

"I am not sure. He keeps his affairs mostly to himself."

A curious look crossed Ames's face, and Rod felt his story weakening. The storekeeper began gathering dry goods and other consumable necessities from his shelves.

"All he needs to do is head due west until he runs into the Shawnee Trail. He can follow that north a ways before heading northwest about half as far before he hits the biggest outfit."

Rod was glad to hear that Ames's tone sounded more like small talk than the instructions he was looking for. He now had a heading, and he dared not ask for more details. He did, however, dare to steal from Ames when his back was turned, pilfering enough candy and small items to make up the difference between what he would need and what he could pay for and stuffing them into his pockets.

It was both daunting and comforting to learn that he was at least a three-day ride from anywhere of consequence. By the time he reached his destination, he'd be so far away that Stuart wouldn't bother seeking him out.

"This is the best I can do for you," Ames said from behind the counter on which the meager supplies were spread.

Rod was grateful for the stolen items that bulged in his pockets.

"It will have to do. I will let Mr. J ... my father know. He will likely send me back for more."

With that, he bade the clerk farewell and shook the final dust of his old life from his feet.

Eager to put some serious distance between Jass and himself, Rod pushed the old horse through the roughest riding he dared. That night, behind a tree line, he rolled out his gunnysack and whatever else he could manage to make a bedroll.

The night was warm and windless in the pines. A billion stars blinked disapprovingly down at him between the trees. He had taken Jass's dowry, he had abandoned his mother and sisters, and he had stolen from Ames. God would surely punish him for his secret sins. Possibly he would be found and beaten again—or worse, tried and hanged as a horse thief. He remembered one of his mother's oft-quoted Bible verses. *For nothing is secret, that shall not be made manifest; neither anything hid, that shall not be known and come abroad.*

He instantly set his jaw at the thought. Who was God to pass judgment on him? Where had God been when Jass had beaten him? When his mother had stood by and let it happen? Where was God when Ames hadn't given him enough to survive for four days?

Winifred, the nag, snorted irritably and began to grow restless. Rod's mind jumped to an image of a panther prowling in the darkness, or Indians sneaking up to scalp him, or ... or the demons that his mother had raved about during one of her more feverish lectures. Demons with talons that hooked the evildoers and dragged them into the abyss.

Hoo-ooh!

Rod bolted upright at the sound and scooted his back against a tree. Winifred whinnied loudly and jerked at her lashings. Rod's eyes darted all over the trees for the source of—there!

Twenty feet above him, two brilliant yellow eyes burned angrily down at him. Rod's eyes widened, flooding his retinas with all the light of the stars and allowing him to see the outline of a great horned owl.

It stared at him as if to say, "I see your actions, and I know your heart."

For several minutes, it stared at Rod, and he stared back, frozen in fear. Then, as if satisfied that the point had been made, it lifted off the branches and swooped over Rod, over the horse, and into the suddenly starless night. Rod sat upright for a few minutes, terrified that the thing might return, before finally slumping back into his bedroll, confident for the moment that he was safe.

Over the next three days, Rod tormented himself unceasingly with imagined scenarios. If he rode too far without seeing a home or fence, he feared that he was going in the wrong direction.

During the night, he imagined teeth and talons behind every noise or worried that rattlers would be attracted to his body heat as he lay on his makeshift bedroll. In order to calm himself, he tried to imagine what kind of life he could make for himself. He would never farm again—that much he knew. He knew a man free of family could make decent money driving cattle to Kansas. He wondered if he could bluff his way into a job like that. He couldn't be fourteen anymore, but that would be easy enough. The real challenge would be hiding his stupidity until he could catch on to the job. Again, one of his mother's Scripture passages came to mind.

Even a fool, when he holdeth his peace, is counted wise: and he that shutteth his lips is esteemed a man of understanding.

Perhaps, if he just kept his mouth shut, no one would know he was a fool.

CHAPTER TWELVE

A New Start

Despite his poor direction, Rod arrived in town halfway through his fourth day of travel. Though far from a metropolis, it was quite the city compared to the little outpost Rod had known his whole life. He meandered slowly for several hours, taking everything in and wondering what wealth could support so many people in one place.

Finding what looked like a general store, Rod secured Winifred and wandered inside. He waited patiently while the storekeeper attended to other guests.

"What can I help you with?"

Rod turned to see a young man not much older than himself. The apron indicated that he must be an apprentice to the storekeeper behind the counter.

"I ... I am looking for the Swagger ranch," he said. "I believe it is around these parts."

The clerk stared at Rod, making him instantly defensive until he remembered that his face was still battered and his nose swollen. He must have been a sight.

"It is south of town, about one mile," the clerk said. "You have business there?"

"Yes ... well, maybe. I am looking for work."

"So, you want to be a cowboy?" A heard-it-a-thousand-times smile spread across the clerk's face.

Rod didn't appreciate the doubting look. "I need a man's job to make a man's living, and I expect the ranch—" he looked around the store to emphasize his point "—is the only place I will find it."

Rod watched with satisfaction as the smile faded from the other boy's face. He rolled his eyes and indicated for Rod to follow him. He approached a wall plastered with posters.

"Anyone who needs help posts it here." He irritably tore down an old ad for a junior clerk position at the general store—which he himself had apparently filled.

He stalked off, leaving Rod to take it all in. Advertisements, want ads, and faces of outlaws spread their news across the length of the wall. As stupid as Rod was, he could read well enough and began searching with fervor until he found exactly what he was looking for—a new-looking advertisement:

Seeking able-bodied men for cattle drive.

Must be able to endure harsh weather and hostile Indians.

Cowboys $35 a month

Wranglers $20 a month

All wages payable at sale of cattle.

A man's past is his past, but his future must be under control.

Drinking or gambling on the trail is not tolerated.

Rod considered asking the clerk how old the ad was and whether the cowboy positions might still be available, but he decided he wouldn't get a satisfactory answer from the boy he'd just insulted. He waited until the junior clerk was engaged with another customer, then approached the storekeeper.

The man all but jumped at the sight of Rod's battered face but recomposed himself smoothly. "Yes sir, how can I help you?"

"Do you know if any positions from this ad are available?" he asked.

"Only way to tell is to inquire at the ranch." He pointed to the bottom of the page, which read:

Inquire within.

"If I were you, I'd ask for Jim. He works for Swagger and is likely the trail boss for this ad."

The man immediately began filling an order for the previous customer. He opened a jar, looked inside, and swore.

"How do I find him?" Rod asked.

"Thomas!" the storekeeper yelled, causing Rod to jump.

The young clerk looked up.

"Quit lollygagging and fill up those canisters!"

The clerk looked first at the storekeeper, then at Rod, who took the opportunity to motion the clerk to action with a wave of his hand. The boy clenched his teeth, huffing into the back of the store.

The storekeeper refocused on Rod. "You were saying?"

"Where do I find Jim?"

"Look for the biggest guy with the biggest beard. *That's* Jim."

Once outside, Rod unhitched Winifred and set course for the ranch.

When he arrived, he found the place in a flurry of activity. It was a big outfit, and the operation was so overwhelming that Rod soon began to doubt he could even pretend to be fit for employment.

With nothing besides the storekeeper's description to go on, Rod wandered the grounds looking for the largest bearded man he could find. He knew without question when he found him.

He sat on a massive horse—at least eighteen hands—but compared to the man, the horse seemed quite normal sized. Even standing, Jim would be a head taller than most. His brown skin betrayed not only a hard life under the sun but an indomitable tenacity. No Texan was appointed boss over white men unless it was deserved. His dark eyes fell on two men standing next to a wooden crate.

"Get that wagon loaded, *now!*" he ordered. "Where is Harold? No, go and *find* him!"

Rod was robbed of the little confidence he possessed. He approached Jim's enormous horse cautiously, not wanting to ruin his chances with a bad impression. Jim jumped, as if suddenly aware of being stalked, then turned impatiently to Rod.

"What do you need?" he asked gruffly.

So much for a good impression. Rod remembered his strategy to keep his foolishness secret.

"I am answering your ad. You still need cowboys?"

He waited to be laughed off and was surprised when the big man asked, “You drove before?”

“A little,” Rod lied.

“Lies. No one droves ‘a little.’ You either done it or not.”

Rod started to panic. Not twenty words in, and he’d already exposed himself as a fool and a liar. Jim eyed him suspiciously.

“Not.” Rod sighed.

“Follow me.”

Rod felt like he was following Stuart to the barn again. He’d done it now. He’d lied to this man, who would not let Rod go without vengeance. Suddenly, he wondered if this could somehow lead to him being discovered as a horse-thieving runaway. His head swam, and it was all he could do to hope that he still at least looked like a man.

In the shade cast by the nearest building, Jim swung out of the saddle and waited for Rod to catch up.

“So, you want to join my drive?”

“Yes ... sir.”

“And you have no experience?”

“No, sir.”

Jim scowled. “Family?”

Rod shook his head.

“How old are you?”

“Nineteen.”

Jim nodded. “You have gear?”

Rod pointed across the way to the fence. “I have a horse and saddle. She is tied up over there.”

Jim followed Rod’s finger and scoffed, and the two sat in silence as the older man contemplated.

Presently, he addressed Rod. "Listen, I ride tomorrow, and I am a man down." He paused as though considering the missing man. "Men who forget to shut their mouths sometimes forget how to breathe ... you understand this?"

Rod nodded, trying his best to appear that he knew this to be a natural rule.

Jim continued. "I have no time to prove you, but any man is better than no man—so long as he keeps his affairs his own and gives me everything else." He chewed for a few moments. "I will take you on as a wrangler. You will prove yourself on the trail. If you survive and are worth keeping, you will be paid fifteen dollars a month, less the gear I must advance you, when we get to Kansas. If you cause me problems, I will leave you wherever I find a replacement, comprende?"

Rod gathered his courage. He had to try, or he'd regret it. "The ad said twenty dollars."

Jim narrowed his eyes at the greenhorn's audacity. "Twenty dollars is for proven men with gear. Advanced gear, no experience, and my desperation all get you more than you are worth. Fifteen."

Rod knew better than to ask for eighteen. He knew little about bartering and even less about this business. The trail boss was right; it was more than he was worth.

Rod held out his hand in silent acceptance. Jim eyed him, solidifying his authority by making Rod wait before finally extending his hand. The point was made. Jim was rolling the dice, and he'd better not be let down.

"What is your name, son?"

"Rod ..." *Wait.* A thought struck him, and a corner of his mouth lifted. "Harper."

CHAPTER THIRTEEN

The Trail

Life on the cattle trail was difficult as a rule, but it was bitterly difficult for Harper, who seemed to make twelve mistakes before finally learning the simplest of tasks. By the end of the first week, he had already misinterpreted hand signals, botched maneuvers, misused jargon, and accidentally usurped the pecking order. He knew that he belonged at the bottom, of course, but it took him some time to differentiate between respect that came by position and that which came from wisdom, strength, and personality.

One example of this was Gerald Lloyd. What Lloyd lacked in position, he made up for with personality. He was brash, funny, and had a knack for rallying the men. Unfortunately for poor Harper, Lloyd's mean temper and charisma made for a miserable combination.

After a grueling five days on the trail, Lloyd addressed Harper in front of the rest of the men.

"What are you doing out here, *Hopper*?" he asked. "You almost caused a stampede, running in between the horns like you did."

Harper said nothing, partially because he was already catching wise to Lloyd's informal authority and partially because Lloyd was a grown man and Harper was still a boy.

Lloyd jerked his head toward Harper. "Boss, why him?"

Jim looked at Lloyd. "Maybe you should have watched Will's mouth for him. Then he would be here—alive—and I would not have had to hire a tenderfoot."

Lloyd turned back to Harper. "You better learn quick, greenhorn, before you get somebody killed." He spat and stalked off toward the wagon.

It was a mercy Jim paid Harper a full five dollars less than the next wrangler; otherwise, he would have been met with mutiny. Wages notwithstanding, nearly every man followed Lloyd's example, making it clear that Harper had no business in their company. With no other recourse, Harper simply stayed quiet and worked hard.

"Do better, be better," he would remind himself.

Harper developed the skills of his trade quickly, and by the time the three-month expedition ended and the men were paid out, he had grown lean and hard muscled, his skill now barely discernible from the old hats'. He would, to them, however, always be the idiot tenderfoot.

There was no way that Lloyd and the others didn't notice his prowess, but for some reason, no one acknowledged it. Few probably cared. Some, including Lloyd, obviously derived pleasure in withholding encouragement, and a few others likely refused to validate Harper for fear of Lloyd's disapproval. Harper, though, could not shake the feeling that there was only one true reason. He was stupid, a liability, and unworthy of praise.

Harper did notice that Jim, though hard on him, was not overtly unkind. Harper wondered if Jim was satisfied with his gamble. After all, he had not been abandoned along the trail. Harper soon dismissed this notion, however, believing instead that Jim simply didn't care enough to make his life difficult. This idea fit best, considering his inability to ever be good enough.

Harper had only made a few dollars after paying the boss for the advanced gear. But he now owned his own tools, most notably his pistol, and enough experience to make him marketable for the next drive.

On the final day of the return home, Jim sidled up to Harper. "Where will you go next?"

"I do not know. I will find another job until your next drive ... if you will have me."

"I have rehired worse," Jim said. "Stick around. I will find work for you at Swagger. It will be neither easy nor profitable, but it will feed and shelter you. If you can stick it out, I will take you on the drive next spring."

The offer should not have surprised Harper. If he had seen clearly, he would have known that he had *earned* this, but instead of the pride and validation that should have followed, he only felt lucky—as though he had cheated and won. Believing you are worthless is a miserable existence indeed. And the hard life that Harper had been dealt was just beginning.

"Do better. *Be* better."

The following year's drive was barely underway when Lloyd, who had also returned, once again made it clear to Harper that he still had no business on their trail. The abuse became worse when Lloyd found out that Harper's wages had increased to the standard rate for wranglers. Jim, content as long as everyone did their fair share, stayed out of the conflict. If they beat his wrangler, he'd step in. Harper, only fifteen, accepted the men's abuse without protest.

"Do better. Be better. Keep your mouth shut," he would whisper to himself.

Nose down, mouth shut, and muscles sore, Harper worked harder than anyone on the trail. His sole purpose was to earn the respect of his peers. They had to have recognized his work ethic, but no one seemed to care or dare mention it.

Toward the end of the drive, a few men began coming to Harper privately during the evening hours, addressing him by his hated nickname and urging him in fatherly tones of mock concern to cut and run.

"You do not belong, Hopper," a second-year cowboy sneered.

"There is no shame in a man admitting his limitations," whispered another.

Sometimes two cowboys would sandwich Harper as they rode the plain. "Listen, you need to quit this outfit before something bad happens."

Even Lloyd, in his more "fatherly" moments, pretended to mentor Harper. "This is dangerous work, and you—you are not a dangerous man."

They were right in that allegation; Harper was not yet dangerous. But he was no quitter. They'd have to kill him first. Even so, soon after entering Kansas, Harper was almost killed—not by his peers, but by landowners defending their property boundaries.

"Leave it alone," Jim said, chewing a stalk of grass and eyeing the new fence. It seemed to stretch for miles across the Kansas plain.

Several of Jim's men, in the middle of removing a section of the fence, stopped.

Lloyd let the timber drop back into place. "But, Boss—it is public land."

"Maybe it is, maybe it is not," Jim returned.

"It was public last year; you are telling me the boundary has changed?"

"I am telling you I do not know. Are you willing to stake your life on it?"

Lloyd cursed, and several others joined him. A fence around public land could be demolished, but there was almost no chance that any farmer or rancher would take the trouble to build a fence around land they didn't own. Either way, touching the fence would likely result in serious trouble.

"If we have to go around, we will go around," Jim said. "Move 'em out."

Four miles into the detour, several cows knocked over the fence and began to graze on the other side. By the time Harper doubled back to move them out, three riders from within the fenced zone were moving in on him. They fired their guns, spooking the herd and causing them to stampede.

Harper, inside the fence line, was still trying to coax the wayward cattle to rejoin the others. "Hyah, hyah!"

Two more riders joined the other three and quickly surrounded Harper, who was mentally caught between wanting to draw his gun and knowing that it would likely be the last thing he ever did. He quickly decided it would be more prudent to hope they could tell he was just trying to remove his cows from their property.

One man stood out from the rest. He wore a gun on each hip but had drawn neither, opting instead to let his companions cover him. He was clearly in charge.

"You are off public lands, drover!"

"It was an accident," Harper said. "We were headed west around the property when these"—he indicated the six remaining cows—"pushed over the fence."

"Lies!" shouted one of the men.

Harper imagined him to be the Lloyd of this group but said nothing. Of course, the man would assume Harper was lying—everyone always did.

Jim and Lloyd rode up, crossed the fence line, and were immediately at gunpoint.

"Hopper, you fool, what are you doing?" Lloyd shouted, obviously happy to use Harper as a scapegoat.

Jim showed his palms and indicated for Lloyd and Harper to do the same.

"Peace," he said. "If we wanted to invade your property, we would have done it four miles east of here. Recognize the situation for what it is, and let us take our leave."

"Take your leave?" said the man in charge. "Why not take your tick-infested mexi-cows back the way you came instead of spreading your disease here?"

"We have a right to be on public land, hombre," Jim said.

"Right now, you are on private property and should be shot. I cannot have your herd infecting mine."

Lloyd opened his mouth, but Jim silenced him with a wave of his hand.

"You have already scattered twelve hundred 'mexi-cows' all over your plains by firing your guns. What do you want, if not to kill us?"

The other man dropped his squared shoulders.

Jim continued. "I would gladly give you the six ..."

One of the cows trotted back onto the public land, and two others followed her.

"... *three* cows that are on your land to appease you, but I know the last thing you want is Texas ticks killing off your herd. Why not call it square and let us be on our way?"

Clever Jim had used the man's rhetoric to his own advantage. The other side's boss man had to either kill them, let them go, or admit that Jim's cattle were good and take the bribe.

"Fix my fence and get out of here." He rode away, motioning for his gang to follow him and leaving Jim, Harper, and Lloyd alone on the plain.

"Dadgum it, Hopper—" Lloyd began.

"Enough!" Jim barked. "Hop—Harper did not *drive* the herd into the fence, and you know it, Lloyd. We have already lost enough time. Join the others and make sure everything is accounted for."

Lloyd spat and galloped off in the direction of the stampede.

Jim turned to Harper. "You bring these back?" He indicated with his head to the six cows who had all regrouped on the correct side of the fence.

"Yes sir. What about the fence?"

"Let them fix their own blasted fence."

From that day on, Lloyd said little to Harper, although he frequently caught Lloyd staring at him from his position on the plain or across the supper circle in the evenings.

Once paid out, the weary group began the long way back to Texas. Harper had decided weeks before that he would not drive with the group again. Jim was fair to Harper, but he allowed the men too much license in abusing him. Harper considered traveling back alone, but there was safety in numbers—hostile though they were. Besides, Harper was a coward. At least that was the lie he told himself. The truth was that he wasn't twenty—he was fifteen—and traveling five hundred miles alone was naturally terrifying to him. He would travel back with them as far as Texas before leaving the group for friendlier territory.

The night after crossing the Texas border, the men celebrated. There was no drinking on the trail, but this wasn't the trail, it was homecoming. Whiskey purchased in Kansas flowed, and challenges flew.

"Grass Hop-per!" Lloyd slurred. "Come here."

He put up his fists, and the revelers closed around them. From behind, someone shoved Harper into Lloyd, and the fists began to fly.

Lloyd's fists, not Harper's.

"Come on, boy, defend yourself," someone called out.

Lloyd boxed the stunned Harper and, with great effort, tackled him to the ground, where he continued to pummel him.

"Come on, big boy! You going to let your daddy beat you like that?"

Everyone laughed and jeered as the memory of Stuart washed over Harper.

That night, after everyone had gone to sleep or simply passed out, Harper gathered up his things and re-saddled Winifred. He stood for a long time, reins in hand, one foot in the stirrup, before securing her and going through the camp. It didn't take long for him to find what he was looking for.

Gerald Lloyd lay next to a pool of vomit. He hadn't even made it back to his bedroll. Harper wanted to kill every last man for taking part—or being complicit—in what had happened. He stooped and examined Lloyd for a moment before nudging the man with his foot.

Nothing.

Harper took one last look around to make sure no one was awake, hauled his boot back as far as he could, and kicked most of Lloyd's teeth out. The man wheezed and gasped but was unable to raise himself. No one else stirred.

Harper quickly stole over to Winifred and rode off into the night alone.

CHAPTER FOURTEEN

Wily Bill

Harper had seen enough of the territory to know where he'd be most likely to find work. After heading toward his best prospect, a small community in north Texas, he found himself at a small ranch looking for a small man. Just as with Jim, Harper knew when he'd found him. In stark contrast to Jim, Bill was not much to look at, but Harper quickly found that what he lacked in physical prowess he more than made up for in cunning.

"You want to work for me?" he asked.

"Yes sir."

"What are your qualifications?"

"I have completed two cattle drives from Swagger to Kansas; I can handle anything here."

Bill narrowed his eyes.

"Why are you no longer droving?"

"I may drove again, but I need work until next spring."

"How old are you?"

"Twenty."

"I usually hire local boys to assist me, but I find myself needing more regular help these days. Do you have a family?"

"No sir."

"Good." Bill contemplated. "I will pay you two bits a week as long as you are worth it."

Harper worked well for Bill. By the time spring came, the national uproar over states' rights and the emancipation of slaves had reached fever pitch. Texas had voted to leave the Union and had once again branded itself a republic. Calls to arms across the nation had extended westward, and the Republic of Texas issued an edict of compulsory military service.

Still only sixteen, Harper was exempt from the draft. He'd never known anyone who owned human property, and he had no education on the delicate balance between federal and state powers. All he wanted to do was to make enough money to provide for himself, and so, without any real goals or ambition, he was content to do chores for Bill until something better came along.

Stories abounded of the men who had volunteered for the Confederacy, and conscription seemed hardly necessary to the settlers on the frontier. However, either due to the overzealousness of the local conscription officer or just plain old bad luck, the day came when Bill was notified that his number was up.

"William Wilson."

Two uniformed men stood outside Bill's shack. One held a paper from which he read.

"You are hereby summoned to report for duty in three days' time at the Confederate States' Army conscription office."

"Give me that!" Bill said, snatching the notice from the conscription officer.

"I am an old man," he protested.

"Is your age on the notice incorrect?"

Bill answered with a withering glare.

"Three days' time, Mr. Wilson."

The two men began to leave.

"Wait!" Bill said.

The men turned back.

"Is there no draft for my hired man? And what is this about a substitution?"

There were any number of ways to escape the draft, but Bill, ever so shrewd, knew that he'd have to cheat someone besides the army if he expected to get away with it.

When hired, Harper had passed himself off as twenty years old, but Wily Bill never believed this to be true. His suspicion gained ground when he managed to find out that Harper had somehow avoided the draft. A plan began to form in his mind.

The following morning, after helping Harper bring a stray heifer around, Bill pulled up next to his employee.

"Let me ask you something, son."

Son? thought Harper. Bill generally either gave orders or left him alone. He immediately tried to figure out what Bill's angle was.

Bill continued. "Why have you not registered with the conscription office?"

Harper tensed. Something was definitely up. "Who says I have not registered?"

"I do ... and I have ways of knowing."

Harper weighed this and decided it was most likely true. He said nothing.

Bill persisted. "Are you yellow?"

Harper bristled. Of course he was yellow, but that was a secret he guarded closely. "No," he answered flatly.

"Why then?"

Harper sighed. "I do not see how this fight concerns me. I own no one."

"It concerns all of us, *boy!*" Bill hissed. "First, the Yankees force rules on our neighbors, and the next thing you know, we might as well be polishing saddles for the redcoats!"

Harper withered under the rhetoric, instantly feeling ignorant and unpatriotic.

Bill warmed to his subject. "Our relations fought a war they could not hope to win to free us from tyranny, a government so far removed from their lives that the laws they levied did not even make sense. Everything my ancestors had belonged to someone else, and now, so will everything of ours!"

Bill had escalated into a shout, but now cut himself off abruptly.

He made a show of checking his emotions before wrapping up his speech.

"I never figured you for a snake, but failing to answer the call? I cannot abide it!"

Harper could not stand the guilt any longer. "I am no snake," he began. "I did not register because I am only sixteen. I lied to you about my age but not to the conscriptor."

There it was, the truth Harper had worked so hard to hide. He had never acted like a man, and now Bill knew he wasn't.

"It was not my intent to connive," Harper lied. "Perhaps I should just tell the conscriptor I lied about my age so I can register."

"Are you out of your mind, boy?" Bill asked. "You would be publicly branded a coward and likely thrown in jail. Although, I am disappointed that you would lie to me so I would pay you a man's wage yet only tell the truth to protect yourself."

Bill was using Harper's own shame against him now. Harper was floundering—caught, as any sixteen-year-old boy, between his desire for the honor given to men and his need for the protection afforded to children.

He huffed in frustration. "I may only have sixteen years, but I support myself and can work as well as any man. If I cannot register for conscription now, I do not know what you would have me do."

Bill allowed Harper to dangle in agony for several minutes before speaking.

"Perhaps," he began cautiously, "there is something of a solution."

Harper waited expectantly, his desire for redemption overwhelming both his distrust for Bill and his fear of an unknown war.

"There are fewer eligible men than you may think," Bill said. "Volunteers have already been taken. I myself planned to volunteer, but I fear for my sister now that her husband has been taken. I have been told I will likely be called up in the next few days, and I cannot leave her to fend for herself."

Harper could not see where Bill was going with all of this but remained patient while the older man continued.

"The only honorable way to attend my familial duties is to find a substitute. So here is my proposal. I will pay you, who have no family, fifty dollars to volunteer as my substitute—if you are a man, as you say. This will put money in your pocket and experience in your head and will keep my sister from starvation. Anyhow, it is likely much safer for you than for me. As you are only sixteen, I expect they will make you a drummer."

Harper was cornered. There was no way out without admitting he was a coward, and he would rather die on a battlefield than for anyone—even Bill—to know he was scared. Besides, fifty dollars was almost as much as he'd made on the last cattle drive. Beyond this, it felt noble to think that his substitution could ensure the safety of Bill's sister—whoever she was. He had no choice.

"Your sister, she cannot provide without you?" Harper asked, pretending this was the only reason he would even consider the proposal.

"She will not survive," Bill replied.

"Then I will go in your stead."

Over the next two days, Bill worked out the details with the conscription officer, stating that he had taken Harper in and was, therefore, owed the title of guardian. Harper committed to his decision, validated that Bill had cared for him and that he was now returning the favor to ensure the safety of Bill's extended family. All too conveniently for Bill, Harper's orders came, and he was required to leave before Bill rendered payment for the substitution. Harper's protests that he needed to speak with Bill before he left were immediately met with accusations of desertion and a threat of severe punishment.

Lucky Wily Bill had simultaneously defended his honor and his lifestyle; he had preserved his ideals and his comfort. Harper was issued a uniform and shoved into duty without ever seeing a dime, and Bill remained safely on his property while other men died for a cause he clearly only pretended to believe in.

CHAPTER FIFTEEN

COMBAT

HARPER WAS ONCE AGAIN a workhorse, this time for the Confederate States Army. Aside from the Gulf region, there was little fighting in Texas, and Harper worked to assimilate into the relatively dull routine of garrison life.

"Boy!" Sergeant Johnson, one of Harper's most antagonistic superiors, yelled.

Harper, who had been walking across the compound toward the mess hall for kitchen duty, changed directions and stood smartly in front of the sergeant.

Johnson smiled wickedly and held out two buckets. "Take these. You are now on latrine duty."

"Sergeant, I have orders for kitchen duty."

"Who gave you orders?"

"Lieutenant Smith, Sergeant."

The sergeant rolled his eyes. "Find me the moment you are released."

"Yes, Sergeant."

Harper resumed his original route and grinned to himself. It was the cook who had ordered him on kitchen duty, but the cook took his orders from the lieutenant so, in a sense, Harper was correct. All he had to do now was get a higher-ranking soldier to order him to do anything other than latrine duty.

He had learned quickly how impossible it was to please everyone. He'd also learned whom he could afford to disappoint and whom he had to obey immediately—the military structure made that part reasonably easy. Once again, he didn't belong and found himself quite alone in the military community of men.

A series of unexpected events in his first year of service landed him across the border in the Indian Territory. His brigade was mostly Seminole Native Americans and a few other soldiers who had enlisted in northernmost Texas. There, they were spread out in picket lines far and wide, doing their best to patrol the plains. Their mission was simple. Keep the Union force from moving south through Texas and into Galveston.

Engagements with the enemy were infrequent but tornadic: unexpected, fierce, and short-lived. Officially, the rules of engagement excluded boys as young as Harper from combat, but since every man counted in battle, no one "officially" objected to his using an unattended weapon when caught in the crossfire.

Harper was desperate to prove his worth and fought fiercely. He knew that he was still a throwaway and wouldn't likely receive accolades for bravery, yet for reasons he did not understand, he could not stop trying.

The truth of the matter was that somewhere within his oxygen-deprived heart, a gasping flame still flickered. A flame of hope that just maybe, if he tried harder than anyone else, he could somehow *do better, be better,* or at least, be enough to earn the respect of men. If others valued him, then there was a chance he could value himself. Had Harper simply acknowledged this truth, he would have quickly realized that *he* was the only man whose approval he needed. But life is cruel, and the seventeen-year-old cloud of worthlessness and shame that had gathered over Harper would hide this truth from him.

Forever.

One morning, gunfire erupted as Harper delivered supplies to the picket line.

Two men near him fell, mortally wounded, and shouts of alarm went up.

Harper gasped in terror and instinctively dropped to the ground. He lay there for several seconds, frozen with fear.

"Do better, Harper," he chided, shaming himself into action.

"Be better!"

He forced himself to quickly check the casualties. One of the men was already dead, the exiting round taking off the back half of his head. The other was alive but bleeding heavily. Harper began working a tourniquet around the soldier's arm as bullets continued to whiz through the air.

"Fall back!" the patrol sergeant yelled amid the gunfire.

Harper suddenly found himself alone with the men. One dead and one dying. He could hear the shouts of the approaching Yankees.

They will be upon me any second. They will bayonet me for sure.

Harper knew his stretcher-bearing status would make no difference. He was wearing the uniform, and neither side had a good track record for taking prisoners.

After grabbing the wounded soldier's musket, he shoved it into the man's hands, hoping he would rally.

"Can you shoot?" he asked.

The man didn't respond.

Harper grabbed the dead man's gun and shouldered it. Staying low, he peered over the edge of the tall grass. Catching sight of a blue Union uniform, he fired. The blue disappeared as a scream echoed against the trees. Fire had been returned, and the element of surprise was gone. Harper had bought himself some time, but he didn't know how much. He flung the musket to the ground and scrambled to the remaining soldier.

"Can you shoot?" he repeated.

"I cannot. I cannot ... *see*," said the man. His face was drained of color; he was in shock.

"Give me your rifle."

Harper took the weapon and listened. Nothing. He took a deep breath and popped up over the grass. He saw a soldier about thirty yards away. Their eyes met for a split second, and the man shouted.

Now that the attack had stalled, Harper felt confident that taking another Yankee down would cause the group to fall back. Knowing guns were trained on his first location, he scrambled a few yards to the right. He took three quick breaths and forced himself off the ground. In one swift motion, Harper rose, aimed, and fired. By the time the Yankee began to swing his aim toward Harper, it was too late. The man fell into the grass, out of sight.

The enemy's shouts grew fainter, and friendly voices grew louder. Harper grabbed the cartridge pouch from the dead soldier's haversack and reloaded in case his position came under fire again. He was shaking, not only from fear but from exhilaration. He felt like a soldier. He felt ... like a man.

The returning rebels ran past Harper and began canvassing the area. After about ten minutes, they returned to Harper's position, where he held the reloaded musket next to two dead soldiers, one missing a scalp, the other with a half-completed tourniquet hanging loosely above his shredded artery.

Private Caskill shook his head. "Get the death cart, boy."

Harper was crushed. Instead of receiving praise for driving off the enemy, he had been told to prepare for the burial of the man he'd failed to save. He knew the men suspected him of letting a man die while seeking the glory of battle. Protesting this would only be seen as excuse making, and without hope of making a case for himself, he simply let them think what they wanted. Although there was no formal discipline, the men's silent disapproval quickly robbed him of his accomplishment.

Unfairness is the way of the world, and Harper knew he had no choice but to accept it. Inside, however, he boiled with rage. Everyone else had scattered, left him to be killed, and only returned after he single-handedly drove back the assault. Had he not *done better, been better?* What did it profit? All it had done was allow these fools to stack up more false evidence against his character. He hated them for running—for giving in to the fear he had resisted—and then accusing *him* of dereliction. It was nothing new for people to enrich themselves at his expense or to treat him like the loser he was, but now, for the first time, *they* were losers. This time *they* had been the ones to fail, and he afforded them no grace.

Several nights later, Harper lay awake enjoying the fallout as Henry Caskill, one of Harper's squad mates, tore apart his knapsack.

"Where is my 'baccy?"

"You smoked it all, you idiot," said Cyrus Filmore, stretching out in his bedroll.

"I did not. It was in my pack this morning."

Harper's foot brushed up against the missing tin in the bottom of his own bedroll.

Caskill really should be more attentive. He'd taken the opportunity to steal the tobacco tin earlier in the day when the other man's back was turned.

Well, he at least should not accuse me of glory seeking when he left it right in my lap.

It felt good to deprive Caskill of his property—to execute justice for the way Harper's comrade had treated him. He brushed away the thought of how petty he was acting. It did not matter; it was a way to make things more bearable to him.

It is less than he deserves. He'd seek revenge on Private Filmore at the next available opportunity.

Over the next few weeks, Harper developed a habit of quenching the flame of vengeance a little at a time by punishing those who had mistreated him. Most of the time, he simply threw the items away so that he wouldn't be caught with them in his possession. The more he stole, the better he felt, and the more he sought opportunities to exact his personal brand of "justice."

Having attempted to soothe his deep wounds with dishonesty, Harper soon found that stealing sundries no longer provided the satisfaction he sought. In a few months' time, he had graduated to sabotage.

At first, it was nettles in Filmore's bedroll or a chunk of cactus in Caskill's boot. However, the day after Sergeant Johnson had beaten him in front of the other soldiers, Harper tampered with the man's musket so that it would not fire. Getting caught would mean a traitor's death, but that only made him more careful. He had become better, and it hadn't mattered. It was time to make his situation better.

A dark craft was replacing his naivety. He was developing an evil cunning that even Wily Bill, the man who sold him into the army, would not recognize.

Not even Harper's conscience was safe. After all, Johnson had threatened to shoot him for doing a better job than the other men under his command. Surely he was entitled to reduce Sergeant Johnson's longevity in exchange for *that*. Fairness, equity, life: these things no longer mattered. If no one sought justice on his behalf, he would seek it for himself.

"Judge not, that ye be not judged. For with what judgment ye judge, ye shall be judged: and with what measure ye mete, it shall be measured to you again." The chaplain closed the worn book and sandwiched it reverently in both hands. "Thus saith the Lord."

"Amen," the parishioners replied.

Harper stood up and headed back to his unit, pleased to have discovered the services. At first, he had been merely drawn to the nostalgia of his mother's Scripture quoting, but he had quickly realized that "catching heaven" was the most defensible way to be left alone for a couple of hours each week—so long as he had not been specifically ordered to perform some chore. Had he been idle anywhere else, he would undoubtedly have caught hell.

"You there! Boy!"

Harper turned to see Chaplain Jenkins approaching him. His dingy white collar matched the worn Bible in his hands. Times were hard in the South, and the lay pastor's visage reflected this well.

Harper chafed at the term "boy" but obediently waited until the senior man caught up to him.

Jenkins appraised Harper. "Son, have you given your soul to Christ?"

The question was predictable. Truthfully, Harper had expected it ever since the chaplain had made eye contact with him during a service the week before.

Harper attempted to avoid lying. "Maybe ... I think so."

"There is no maybe. You either have or have not."

"I suppose not," Harper admitted.

"Why not? The best time is now."

Harper fidgeted. Why couldn't he just lie?

"Have the other men in my unit given themselves to God?"

Jenkins smiled. It was a kind smile and stood in stark contrast to his angry sermons. "Most of them have, yes. At least, all those who attend services have."

"Those men are hateful to their own," Harper blurted. "How can God accept them?"

It was a spasm of rare honesty brought about by the idea that Caskill, Filmore, Johnson, and others who attended Sunday services now belonged to a righteous God.

"God accepts the man, not the sin."

Harper worked to control his temper, which threatened disrespect toward Jenkins. "I cannot see the difference from where I stand," he admitted.

"I suppose that is part of what makes him God—it is his nature to love the sinner while detesting the sin ... even yours."

Harper scowled. He had no answer. God was God, and he was not, yet that knowledge was a far cry from helping him understand why a just God could allow such injustice in Harper's own life.

For the first time in his life, Harper had an opportunity to seek the guidance he needed to change his course. Unfortunately, unable to make peace with God's seemingly diametrically opposed qualities of justice and mercy, Harper contented himself by using the chaplain's fiery rhetoric to justify the judgment *he* measured out against his fellow soldiers.

Harper rather enjoyed the idea of fire and brimstone. He didn't necessarily buy into heaven or hell, choosing instead to cherry-pick the pieces of the sermon that most resonated with him and wrap them around his own ideals and desires—not unlike the hypocrites who listened attentively on Sunday and then abused him on Monday. Today's message further validated his vindictiveness. He now had biblical license to mete out judgment upon those who judged him. Indeed, Harper now saw himself as an executor of righteous justice.

CHAPTER SIXTEEN

The First

"Gentlemen, say hello to Private Doyle Hill." Captain Feral looked at Harper and the rest of his motley crew of bedraggled and filthy men. "Private Hill is our replacement for Huston and Jessop."

He stopped, letting reality sink in. They had lost two men and now only had one to replace them. The Confederacy was weakening, and everyone was catching on.

"Private Hill!" Captain Feral yelled.

"Yes, Captain."

"Are you ready to kill Yankees?"

Doyle hesitated. Then, as if forcing himself to rally, he gave an unconvincing rebel yell, which was quickly drowned out by the yells of the rest of the company.

Doyle acclimated easily to the social climate of his company, seemingly content to leave others to their business so long as they did the same. Besides his quiet demeanor, the only thing that set him apart from the other men was that he did not join them in treating Harper like a stray dog. It was as though he deemed it unfair and therefore wrong.

After the Indian raid—through which Harper had slept and for which he was subsequently punished—Doyle shared food with him.

"Here, take this—do not let anyone see."

"Thank you, Hill—you are a fool, but thank you."

"Just wolf it down."

A man without food was a man without strength. A man without strength was a dead man.

Harper gravitated to the first friendliness he'd seen since leaving home, and the two became friends—after a fashion—in that Doyle looked out for Harper, and Harper did almost anything he could to repay the kindness.

The more Harper observed Doyle, the more he liked him. He was a strong loner who didn't fall into the same habits of other men. It was as though he did what he wanted without concern for what others thought—a notion that Harper idolized.

"How old are you, Hill?" he asked one night when they were alone.

"Twenty-seven," came the laconic reply.

Harper decided he would have to be direct if he wanted any real insight into his new friend. "Do you disagree with the war, Hill?"

Doyle stared at Harper as though deciding how much information to give away.

"I have seen enough killing," he said finally, then added, "I had no design for combat adventure … but I suppose the Conscription Act disagreed."

"If you disagree with the war, it would be simple enough to leave and go into hiding," Harper pressed.

Doyle gave Harper an admonishing look. "Desertion is wrong, which means serving is right. That is why I wear this uniform. I wish to kill no one, and I find that many who go on about honor or moral agenda are only fooling themselves."

Harper understood. Doyle relied on his conscience for moral decisions, and his pragmatic philosophy gave him license to look no further than his own feelings to determine right and wrong. Moral depravity aside, it was not so unlike Harper's thoughts on right and wrong.

One cold morning as Harper hurried back from the latrine, Doyle grabbed him by the shoulder and marched him some distance from the camp. Once they were out of earshot, Doyle whirled fiercely on his companion.

"What do you think you are doing?"

Harper was caught off guard. He did not handle surprises like this very well and began to stammer. "I … wh-wha-what?"

"I saw you last night!" Doyle hissed, "I will ask again, and do not take me for a fool. What were you doing with the captain's gear?"

Harper's mind raced. How had Doyle seen him? He was sure everyone had been asleep when he crept outside the officer's tent and replaced a few cartridges in his haversack with some he had rigged. That night, he had graduated from tampering with equipment to make it fail, to modifying a cartridge so that it would explode in the barrel when fired. Harper knew this was a new level of evil, but the officer needed to be punished—for lack of leadership, for an inability to control his men, and for abusing and humiliating him. Even so, Harper wasn't sure if it would actually work, and somehow, that made it a little easier for him to carry out his plan.

"I was stealing tobacco from his kit."

Doyle's eyes narrowed. "I do not believe you."

"It is true. He carries a different blend than everyone else, and I wanted to try it."

"This is not the first time you have done this. You are not as clever as you think, and it will get you killed."

Of course he wasn't clever. He was an idiot and a coward. Too weak to stand up for himself and too stupid to carry out justice. Harper felt like a child again, forced by his mother to confess a sin that was already exposed.

"This is, however," Doyle continued, "the first time you have done it to the captain. Look me in the eye and tell me it is not because he raked you over the coals the day before."

Harper said nothing.

Doyle looked around, then refocused on Harper. "He punished you to keep discipline, teach you a lesson, and set an example. This—"

"That was *not* discipline!" Harper blurted out more loudly than he meant to. His justice system was under fire, and he was angry. "I mete out far less than they deserve, Doyle! You have not seen half what I endure! I wear a soldier's uniform, serve with honor, never quit working, and day after day, I am treated like a flea-bitten rat!"

He was shouting now. Shouting at the only friend he'd had since he could remember. "It never changes! It never gets better! Nothing works! I settle accounts this way because there is no justice! I do this ... to escape ... madness."

He fell silent, hoping he'd not overdone it, hoping no one else had heard him, hoping Doyle couldn't see the tears he held back, and hoping against hope that he hadn't destroyed his only friendship.

When people lose their minds, it is best to let them burn themselves out. Doyle remained silent for a few minutes, waiting, as Harper imagined, to see if he was done losing his mind. He fixed his gaze on his friend.

"If this—stealing from a man who does his job—is justice ..." he paused. "Who can stand, Rod?"

"Those who are righteous will stand. Evil must be punished. Leaders without accountability are unfit to lead. A compass without a true north is worthless." Harper was feeling pious once again.

"A compass that points to what cannot be reached is worthless," Doyle retorted.

Harper was silent.

After another minute, Doyle sighed. "Listen, if you are fool enough to risk stealing from Johnson or Filmore, I will look the other way only because it truly is less than they deserve. The captain is different. He is not wrong in this matter. He is also your commanding officer, which means a far worse punishment if you are caught. I cannot let that happen ... to you."

Harper was ashamed. Not for what he had done but for what Doyle knew—or at least what he thought he knew. Doyle did not understand the importance of justice and could not understand that Harper was righteous. But, even after this, Doyle still cared for him. Determined not to endanger their friendship, Harper resolved to curb his vengeance as much as he could stand. This was not *doing better, being better*. Doing better now meant pursuing justice against the unrighteous. Temporarily behaving according to Doyle's standards was merely a way to escape unintended consequences.

Harper's attempt to behave himself came to an unexpected halt when, three days later, the company came under attack.

"Form ranks!" Feral shouted at the stunned soldiers. "Move!"

Unlike the skirmishes experienced over the past two years, this was a planned assault. The Union side deployed a pair of howitzers with explosive shells, sending the men into a panic as the rounds burst overhead.

The men scattered, laying down uncoordinated fire onto the hillside, that the opposing force occupied.

Captain Feral's gun, loaded with Harper's rigged shells, did not explode but failed to discharge. Moments later, a piece of shrapnel tore through his left eye, killing him instantly.

The battle raged for almost half an hour before the rebels fell back in retreat. As the enemy advanced, Harper first searched for Sergeant Johnson and, not seeing him, looked around for an abandoned weapon. There was none he could safely get to, and he decided to keep low until the opportunity came for either attack or retreat.

As the company fell back, Harper could see a few dozen men wounded or killed. During a break in the fire, he began a careful retreat, nearly falling backward over Johnson, who was clutching his leg.

"They are upon us, boy."

Harper stared at the sergeant, a strange feeling coming over him. Here was the man who had caused him more trouble than anyone else since Bill had enslaved him to the Confederates—helpless, bleeding, scared.

Johnson was in pain but seemed irritated by the way Harper crouched, looking at him like he was some sort of sideshow.

"My gun, you *idiot*! Get the gun! *Shoot* them!"

In that moment, Harper made up his mind. He looked around to see if anyone—enemy or friendly—was around. Judging them to be alone, he smiled at his superior.

"I will not. I am not a soldier. I will not defend you now so you can shoot me later for touching a gun."

The color in Johnson's face immediately returned as he boiled into a rage.

I will not shoot you, you ... insubordinate idiot!

Harper leaned in. "Liar."

Johnson began to swear, calling Harper all the usual names. He waited—as he'd seen Doyle do—until the sergeant had burned himself out. He glared furiously at Harper.

Harper leaned over him and put his finger to his lips. Johnson became quiet, as though trusting that Harper had heard someone and was trying to save him by keeping him quiet. Harper swung his leg over and straddled him.

Johnson's eyes bulged. "What the ... ? Get off—"

"Shhhhh," Harper reminded.

Fear flashed in Johnson's eyes, belying his sudden realization of Harper's intentions. Panic replaced his bluster as Harper's big hands closed around his neck, his thumbs pressing hard into his windpipe. The harder Johnson struggled; the tighter Harper gripped. Johnson began to thrash, and Harper throttled his head into the ground.

The two men held each other's gaze until Johnson began to fade, and as the life left his eyes, Harper saw Stuart in his hands. He squeezed so hard he thought his hands would burst through the flesh of Johnson's neck. He strangled Stuart; he choked Bill; he squeezed the life out of every man on the cattle drives, every soldier who abused him, the mother who abandoned him. It was the ultimate justice. In those moments, Harper didn't care if the entirety of both armies overran him. Nothing mattered except knowing sweet, beautiful justice was his.

Harper rolled off the lifeless man, exhausted but intensely satisfied. He let his senses return. The ordeal had lasted only minutes, but it felt like an eternity. Harper was vindicated. He would never be scolded, beaten, or treated like a dumb boy by the sergeant again, and now, as Harper imagined it, Johnson felt the first blinding flames of hell and cursed the man who had sent him there.

Knowing he needed to move fast before the enemy reached him, Harper began to run toward the direction of the retreat, keeping as low as was practical. He stumbled onto several dead and wounded rebels who had been too close together when the howitzer shells exploded.

Remembering that he'd seen Doyle nearby before the fighting

started, he began searching, stepping over the dead and ignoring the wounded once sure they weren't who he was looking for. Some of them called out to him repeatedly for help as he moved past. A hand grabbed his ankle, causing him to fall to the ground. He whirled to see Filmore's bloodied face looking into his eyes.

"Wait! Harper! Help me out ... please!"

So now he was "Harper." He had a name now that he held the power to save. It was worse than if Filmore had just called him "boy" again. Fil's sudden acknowledgment that he was worthy of being called by name repulsed Harper. Only sheer desperation, only imminent death, could motivate Fil to exercise the most common decency of addressing Harper by name. He reared back his free leg and kicked Fil as hard as possible.

"Git off!"

His ankle free, Harper jumped to his feet. He savored the betrayal on Filmore's face as he sucked the dirt off his lip and spat. Without ceremony, he turned around and continued his search while Fil continued to cry out.

A minute later, Harper saw Doyle sitting on the frosted ground. He didn't appear to be wounded, but he didn't move either. Harper approached him carefully, not sure what to make of it. Doyle stared straight ahead, shell-shocked. Harper grabbed him by the shoulders and shook.

"Come on! We have to move!"

Nothing.

"Doyle, get up!"

Nearby, a corpse sputtered and came to life. The man reached for them. It was Caskill. His leg was askew, and he must have been knocked unconscious when a howitzer shell exploded nearby.

"Do ... not ... leave!" He coughed, then continued. "Take me w ... take ... with you! *Doyle!*"

Doyle blinked as he heard his name again. There was no time left. Harper grabbed Doyle and hauled him away as the panicked man shouted after them.

"Come baaack!"

CHAPTER SEVENTEEN

Postbellum

Indian Territory
Spring 1865

Harper saw no significant engagement after the lost battle, during which he killed a man, left one to die, and saved yet another. Soon after, the war ended, and Harper and his company were informed that the winners had taken all. The South had been defeated, and the CSA disbanded.

A smartly dressed Union officer accompanied by his aide-de-camp addressed Harper and his company. "President Lincoln has issued clemency to the rebels, but there will be no eligibility for veterans' entitlements."

There was no reaction from the bedraggled men, some of whom sat on the ground, some of whom leaned on rifles. No one stood at attention. The once-captain who had replaced Feral stood with them, stripped of all authority.

There would be no pensions, no benefits, no mustering-out pay, and no families welcoming either Doyle or Harper. They had their freedom, everlasting shame, and nothing more.

"What next, Hill?" Harper asked.

"I do not know."

Harper brightened. "We should drove together. I was talking to Grier at the saloon—"

"No."

"Why not? What else are you going to do?"

"I will not drove. I will find something else," Doyle replied.

Harper noticed that Doyle hadn't been himself since the battle. Defeat hung on his shoulders. What others saw as shock, Harper recognized as shame, for he, too, knew it well. He knew enough of Doyle to know that he felt that saving others was right; being paralyzed by fear was wrong—and he knew Doyle loathed himself for it. He had always been reserved, but now he was downright hermetic. To Harper's surprise, however, Doyle still somehow generated the courage to pick himself up and move on.

Harper, on the other hand, went back to work, taking the first job he could find, merely existing, and waiting for something better to come along. More than anything, he waited to see what Doyle would come up with in hopes of being invited along.

Meanwhile, Doyle spent his time poring over newspapers and advertisements seeking, as he told Harper, "opportunities out West." Harper didn't care for "out West," but after realizing that when Doyle wasn't completely buried in his research, the loneliness and shame drove the man into depression, Harper did his best to leave him be until he could no longer abide Doyle's mood. Having taken all he could stand of his friend's isolation, Harper decided to drag Doyle out of the boarding house for a little recreation.

"Doyle, let us have a little whiskey."

"No, thank you."

Harper sighed. "Have you not finished reading that paper a hundred times over?"

Ignoring the question, Doyle pointed at the paper. "Look at these advertisements about California gold."

"*That's* what you are spending all your time reading about? Are you going to California? Surely all the good gold has been claimed by now."

"All gold is good gold. Surely there is enough left for me to seek my fortune."

Harper sighed. "Why this? Why gold? Why California? Why not cattle driving ... here?"

"There is nothing for me here, Harper."

Harper scowled. It was a weak answer, and Doyle's expression told him there was more. Did Doyle just not trust him with anything of depth? Did he think Harper was too stunted to process any problems besides his own?

"Suit yourself. I have earned a drink. Maybe I will have one for you as well."

It was in the midst of all this turmoil after Harper had suffered about as much as he could stand, that Doyle met Annie.

CHAPTER EIGHTEEN

Annie

"Can I help you ... ma'am?"

Annie gave a small jump and looked over her shoulder. She then turned back to her task at hand: wrestling a wheel that was threatening to dislodge from her cart and inevitably dump her produce out onto the road. She slammed her shoulder precisely into the wheel, knocking it back on the axle, and neatly dropped the linchpin in place.

Doyle was impressed. She stood up and faced him as she dusted off her dress. Doyle tried not to fidget as she examined him. She almost seemed amused.

"Hattak nukhaklo."

This caught Doyle off guard. Almost all the Native Americans in this area spoke English, and he had expected her to be no different.

"I ... uh ..." Doyle stammered, then, more loudly than he anticipated, blurted, "Do you speak English?"

She looked at him with mock bewilderment.

"Eenglish?" she inquired. Then, satisfied at Doyle's obvious discomfort, replied, "Yes. I speak English."

After stifling as long as possible, she began to laugh. Doyle felt like an idiot, and although he wanted to be annoyed with her, he had to admit she had played him well. Despite trying to deprive her of the satisfaction of her joke, he now found himself laughing.

Annie rubbed the shoulder she'd used to knock the wheel into place. "It is nice to be asked," she said. "I have fixed it, though."

"I am Doyle Hill."

"Annie."

Doyle gave her a quizzical look. "Just ... Annie?"

"Yes. Just Annie."

"That is your school name?"

She blew a wisp of hair from her eyes. "Yes ... before that I was called Nita."

It was as Doyle suspected. Most Choctaw children were assigned Anglo names upon entering the territory schools. Doyle, ever practical, felt that arbitrarily renaming someone was unfair—both to the individual and their family.

"I like both. Which do you prefer?"

She smiled. "I am used to Annie."

The next day, as Annie traveled past Doyle and Harper's boarding house with her vegetable cart, Doyle ran into her again—this time on purpose.

"Hello, Miss Annie."

"Hello, Mr. Hill."

"A little late to be traveling to market, no?" he asked.

Annie tossed her head and blew at the seemingly ever-present wisp of hair that had once again settled over her face. She set the handles of her handcart on the ground. "Late has no meaning when the work never ends."

"Do you work through your dreams?"

"Always." She cracked a smile, and Doyle followed.

"Where do you live?" They both spoke simultaneously, and Doyle laughed—genuinely but also nervously. He did not want to be accused of flirting.

"I am staying at a boarding house for a bit," he answered. "I will soon head West to prospect for gold. How about you?"

"I ... have a place," Annie lied, not wanting to explain why she had no family or home.

"You live with your family?" Doyle said.

"I am ... alone."

Doyle never considered himself the marrying type, but once the idea occurred to him that they might each improve their material and emotional poverty by starting life over together, his mind was made up. He did not love Annie, nor did he have any reason to believe that she loved him, but it still seemed like a decent proposal. Doyle would not simply ask for her companionship—it wouldn't be right. She was no brothel girl, and he wasn't looking for physical comfort. Ignorant in the ways of women and courting rituals, and with the prime time for his journey drawing near, Doyle decided to just ask Annie if she'd like to marry him and move out West.

He assured himself that it wouldn't impact him if she turned him down, but, truthfully, he would've been sorely disappointed to miss an opportunity for close friendship. If she rejected him, he'd leave the next day with Harper. If she accepted, he'd allow her to get her affairs in order before striking out.

On the day of his proposal, Doyle purchased the necessaries to get himself and Harper to California—or at least halfway if Annie came—settled his local accounts, and busied himself to put, as was his way, the conversation with Annie out of his mind entirely until the time came.

It was late afternoon when he saw her along her route. Without a way to ease in to the subject, he approached her directly. She looked up at him and smiled pleasantly.

Doyle tried not to think of how his proposal would play out but could not keep the questions from creeping into his consciousness. Did she enjoy their time together over the past week? Did she have any expectation that their relationship would continue? If she stayed, would she wonder about the sad man she met after the war? Was he worth remembering?

Doyle took a deep breath. "Hello, Miss Annie."

"Hello, Mr. Hill."

He put off the question for a bit. This may be the last time he saw her, and he wanted to at least try to enjoy it. "Have you eaten today?"

"I have had a little," she said simply.

“I have too much.” Doyle threw down his sack and sat on the side of the road. “Share it with me.”

“When have you ever had too much?” she questioned suspiciously.

Doyle considered his response. “Since I bought enough for you to have dinner with me. Here. Now.”

“Aha.” She chuckled, sitting beside him. Then, somewhat uncomfortably, she added, “It is too kind.”

“It is nothing to buy a little time with you. I may leave tomorrow.”

She straightened up. “How is it ... that you *may* leave tomorrow? Will you or will you not?” she asked.

Doyle had not committed, and Annie was too quick to pick up on it.

Nothing for it now.

“I suppose it depends.” He waited to see if she would bite.

Annie watched him stoically.

“It depends on whether or not you will come with me.”

The air became heavy, with Doyle’s last words hanging in the thickness of it. He had cut to the chase, and Annie was completely unprepared.

“What—” She stopped short, as though unsure how to finish. “Why are you asking? What do you want with *me*?”

Doyle, however, afraid that he had insulted her honor, jumped in to clarify. “No, let me be clear. I will not take advantage of you. It is just ...”

He searched for the words—the right words—any words.

"I feel something of a ... kinship ... with you. There is a trust here that I have not known, and ... I do not want to leave it behind."

Annie remained quiet, so Doyle continued to fill the silence.

"We do not know each other well, but I feel that we can be good to each other. I will marry you, Annie, if you will have me. I expect we will come together as married folks do in time, but I will not force you. Anyhow, there is nothing for either of us here anymore."

He'd said all that was needed—more than he'd wanted—and now he fell silent. The two of them sat there, Doyle realizing the gravity of what he had proposed and wondering what sense Annie would make of it. His shame rose like floodwaters. He never should have said anything; he should not have trusted himself to ask, trusted her not to reject him, trusted ... fate ... to provide anything good.

Each minute seemed like an hour. Finally, Doyle decided to leave her with his portion of dinner, grab his bag, and leave. He began wrapping up his food. He would miss this simply beautiful woman.

"I will."

It was so quiet that he wasn't sure he'd heard right. He looked at Annie, who returned his gaze.

She seemed very small and a little frightened. "I know nothing of traveling across country or of mining ... but I will go with you."

He breathed in for what felt like the first time in hours; and again, he was at a loss for words. He decided not to shoot for eloquence.

"That is good to hear. I am glad."

"What happens next?" she asked, catching Doyle unprepared yet again.

"I suppose we will figure it out tomorrow."

CHAPTER NINETEEN

Gold Rush

THE DAY AFTER HIS proposal to Annie, Doyle approached Harper, who was busy drinking his wages away in the saloon. His job, loading wagons, paid him enough to enjoy two glasses of whiskey a week after room and board.

Doyle pushed through the saloon doors, letting them swing in his wake. "Rod, I have news!"

Harper raised his glass to Doyle and let the whiskey fumes burn his throat before speaking. "Let me hear it, Hill."

"Instead of drinking my wages, I have saved enough to finally quit this place and head West."

"And what will you do alone with all your gold?"

"Well ... I have taken a wife."

Harper's jaw dropped. "You *what?*"

Harper had expected the announcement about heading West, but taking a wife? It was a familiar pain—someone he needed now trading him for a spouse. It didn't matter that he had tried to prepare for the possibility that Doyle might not invite him; to have it happen this way was particularly devastating.

Why had he stayed in this god-forsaken, war-ravaged territory, waiting for Doyle to realize he needed to do something with his life? He should have cut and run after Doyle turned down Joe Grier's offer to drove. It would have provided handsomely for them both. Now, having lost the best financial opportunity afforded him, Harper was, once again, to be left on his own. He was trapped between the fury of righteous anger and the heartbreak of an abandoned child, and all of this, all these thoughts, all these feelings took place in the five seconds between Doyle's marriage announcement and his next sentence.

"Her name is Annie. She will be joining us on the trail. You will be coming with us, right?"

If Doyle had perceived Harper's race from steady-state anxiety to a raging inferno to calm lake surface, it certainly would have been a warning sign. If Harper had not already cultivated the habit of justifying his feelings, it too would have been a helpful warning. At that time, however, all Harper knew was that he felt like he'd finally found his place in life. He had friendship, surrogate parents even, and a purpose to set his sights on.

"Tell me, old dog, is she beautiful?"

"She is pretty," Doyle affirmed, "but it is her nature that is truly beautiful."

Harper cocked an eye. "I have never heard you speak like that, Hill. What is so beautiful about her nature?"

Doyle was obviously uncomfortable, but that was okay with Harper. It served him right for eloping.

Doyle squared himself. "She is genuine and ... forgiving. It is, in its own simple way, beautiful."

A week later, Doyle, Annie, and Harper, along with two horses and a wagon, rolled out of the Indian Territory. Doyle estimated that the trip would take between four and six weeks, and just as they had securely lashed all their provisions to the wagon, all three of them prepared their minds for the long trip ahead.

Somewhere around the western border of New Mexico, the wagon bumping and swaying against the hard-packed desert soil, Harper and Annie attempted a game of cards as Doyle drove.

Harper threw down his cards in mild frustration. "I cannot win this game!"

Annie grinned and began to shuffle the deck. Doyle, at the reins, smiled secretly. He had won the jackpot with Annie—she was kind, strong, self-sufficient ... and clever.

"Where did you find this woman?" Harper asked Doyle.

"I found *him*," Annie answered.

Harper, pretending not to trust Annie, grabbed the cards from her and began to shuffle the deck himself. "Where are we, anyway?"

"I think we have seen the last of the New Mexico Territory," Doyle said. "This is most likely the Arizona Territory."

"Look!" Annie pointed to an object in the distance up ahead.

Harper stood, almost lost his balance, steadied himself by grabbing onto Doyle's shoulder, and strained his eyes. Doyle said nothing. He had noticed the wagon twenty minutes ago.

"There's another," Harper said.

Annie and Doyle both turned toward Harper and followed his finger across the wasteland to a caravan of two wagons and several horses grouped far behind them.

"We should find out where they are headed," Annie suggested. "There is safety in numbers."

"More people means more trouble," Doyle muttered.

Over the next few hours, the caravan behind them drew closer, and Doyle—with dread—began to realize it was only a matter of time before the group would overtake them. He could not speed up or he would overtake the slower wagon in front of them. Socialization was inevitable.

By the late afternoon, the eastern group overtook them, the first wagon driver calling out as they pulled abreast.

"Ho there!"

"Ho!" called Annie, waving happily.

The second wagon pulled alongside to the right of the Hill's, trapping poor Doyle between the two schooners.

"Where are you going?" asked a younger man driving the second wagon.

"California," Harper answered. "And you?"

"The same," shouted the first driver over the din of hooves, wheels, and rattling supplies. "We plan to prospect for gold. Where are you camping?" he asked Doyle.

"We will pull off once it becomes too dark to see."

"Darkness is only an hour or so away," the man said. "You are welcome to circle up with us if you like—for safety."

Doyle did not like this, but of course, Annie did. Harper was ambivalent, and Annie won the day.

That night, having overtaken the westernmost wagon, which was driven by two men, the three groups prepared camp for the night.

Once things had settled, Annie took it upon herself to make introductions.

"I am Annie. This is my ... husband, Doyle, and his partner, Rodney Harper."

Doyle nodded a silent greeting.

"Harper," Rod said, "please."

"My name is Jack," said the driver of the first wagon, a man in his mid-fifties. "And this—" he put his arm around a woman who matched him almost perfectly, "is my wife, Marie."

Marie set her darning needles in her lap and waved to the group good-naturedly. "Hello."

"Junior," the second driver touched his chest. He was a well-built man not much older than Harper. He looked toward the woman next to him. "This is my wife, Samantha. And those two—" he indicated the two children playing nearby, "are my boys. Earnest is the older—he's the one whittling—and the younger is Ethan."

"How do you know Jack and Marie?" Annie asked Samantha.

"They are Junior's father and mother," said Samantha. "We used to run a farm together—before the war took it."

All eyes fell on the two men from the foremost wagon.

"Wilfred," said one of them, a lanky man with a cowboy look. He pointed to a short man—in every way Wilfred's opposite—who was busy rolling a cigarette. "This here is Gilbert."

"Where is everyone from?" asked Jack. "We ourselves are coming from Mississippi—looking for a new start after the war."

"We left from the Indian Territory, but Doyle and I are from Texas," Harper said.

"Are you from the territory?" Samantha asked Annie.

"Yes," Annie answered. "That is where I met Doyle."

"What about you, Gilbert?" Jack asked.

Gilbert struck a match. "We are from Louisiana."

"And what brings you out West?"

"Gold," he replied, "same as everyone else."

The conversation hit an awkward lull as Gilbert and Wilfred began to share the cigarette.

Jack lit a pipe. "Anyone have any trouble on the trail?" he asked after a few moments.

Harper looked up. "What kind of trouble?"

"Oh, you know, broken wheels, rattlesnakes ... bandits—anything that makes for a good story."

Junior grinned.

"We had a wheel give us some trouble, but it was nothing Annie could not fix," Harper offered.

Doyle smiled at Annie, remembering how handily she'd fixed her cart the first time he met her on the road.

"But besides that, our travel has been uneventful," said Annie, looking to Doyle and Harper.

Harper nodded.

"I wish we could say the same," Samantha said. "So many of those we have passed so far have been very distrustful—some of them have been downright mean."

"Why?" asked Harper.

"They are all afraid everyone who passes them is going to stake the last good claim," Junior said.

"It is true," said Jack. "They act like only a single claim is left in all of California."

"Some of them are even sabotaging other people to try to take them off the trail," Marie said, her eyes on the two reticent men by the front wagon.

Wilfred and Gilbert were too busy whispering to each other to notice. Doyle decided to keep an eye on them tonight and try to separate from them at first light tomorrow. They were shifty, and they were slow. If anyone was going to be capable and motivated of hamstringing another traveler, it would be them.

Doyle didn't want to have the nightmare again, and he didn't want to leave anyone unwatched. Fear and mistrust meant no sleep.

A movement in the dark caught his eye. Slowly and carefully, Doyle turned his head and peered into the darkness. Someone was moving toward the horses. It was a man—wait—two men! Most likely Wilfred and Gilbert. Doyle knew they could just be quietly leaving, but that didn't make sense to him. Why would they wait till the middle of the night to sneak away unless they were planning something sinister?

He waited until he could be sure of foul play. When he saw them untie a third horse, he knew something was wrong but was unable to confront them. He knew they'd never escape undetected, and that was what scared him the most. What if they weren't planning on sneaking away? What if they planned to kill them all and rob them? Doyle slowly and carefully sat halfway up but could not get himself to go any farther.

Come on! Come on!

Suddenly, Doyle heard a hammer click back, then another.

"Going somewhere, fellas?"

Jack and Junior had apparently had the same concern as Doyle.

With no good story to tell, the two guilty men put up their hands.

"No, no, no," Junior warned, "tie the horses back up before they wander."

"Your horses, too," said Jack.

Doyle got up, as did everyone besides Harper and the children.

Doyle helped Jack and Junior relieve the other two men of their weapons.

"You have forfeited your weapons," Jack told them. "They now belong to us—as should your lives for trying to steal horses. You are lucky my grandsons are here, or I would have shot you where you stand."

"You should have shot us, old man." Wilfred sneered. "You're too soft to survive the gold horde. They will cut your throats as you sleep!"

The hair on Doyle's neck pricked up.

"Maybe you are too stupid to survive," said Junior, moving closer to Wilfred.

He stared at Wilfred, silently asking for a reason to pull the trigger. After a few moments, his point made, he addressed both men.

"Remove your boots," he ordered.

Glaring at Jack and Junior, the men did as they were told.

"Now march, boys."

"Where?" Wilfred asked.

"I do not care where, but if I see you again, I will shoot you," Jack said. "I suggest you do not return to your wagon until noon. I also suggest you do not catch up to us."

The two men retreated, unarmed and unshod, into the darkness. Jack grabbed their boots and hurled them away into the desert night.

"That ought to slow them down," Jack said with satisfaction.

"And this ought to speed their retreat," said Junior, firing two shots in the direction of the men.

"Nyuh?" Harper awoke suddenly.

"Come on, Doyle," Jack said. "Let us lash their horses to their wagon and head out. Dark or not, we need to leave now."

"Gold horde," Junior scoffed.

Jack sighed. "I think he is right, son. Gold does terrible things to weak people. I doubt we have seen the last of their kind."

Doyle refused to camp with anyone else after that night. In fact, the more he thought about greedy people clamoring for unproven claims and squabbling over what little could be found, the more he disliked the idea of gold prospecting. Still, they had come too far to do nothing. During his research, he had learned about silver mining, but had initially discarded it—why hunt silver if you can find gold? Now, however, if everyone thought as he had, perhaps looking for a silver lode would be less competitive.

"Annie, Harper, I do not want to go to California," Doyle confessed one evening.

Harper looked up with alarm.

"Doyle ... what would you have us do?" Annie asked. "We have traveled nearly a thousand miles, to the middle of the desert!"

"I am not suggesting we go back," he said, "only that I cannot place us in such danger now that I know it exists."

"Should we ... ranch?" Harper asked. "Because if we do that, then we would be better off in Tex—"

"I want to head north into Nevada and prospect for silver. We can do so with less ... madness. If we strike, then we will keep it to ourselves—no matter what."

The group passed through the popular areas in southern and central Nevada and meandered north until finding Weston. From there, Doyle led them farther north to ensure solitude before searching for months in the sparse landscape, looking for any sign of silver lode. To keep them from starving, Annie began diligently gathering and gardening. It was what she knew, and, right then, it was what they needed.

The following spring, a bedraggled and gaunt Doyle finally accepted that he could no longer live on dreams any more than he could survive his nightmares—which the stress of survival had greatly aggravated. He was responsible for his family, and he alone bore the responsibility for their situation. Doyle's sense of responsibility at last won out and he once and for all abandoned prospecting, turning his attention instead to building a small cattle herd. After all, it was what he and Harper knew, and, right then, it was what they needed.

By the end of their second year on the failed silver claim, Harper and the Hills began to see more people in the area. The Central Pacific Railroad had reached Weston and exploded it into a city. Over the next five years, the Hill ranch grew to the point that Doyle, Annie, and Harper could survive comfortably.

Initially, they lived in two small huts, but as their situation improved, the Hills traded their sod hut for a timber cabin, complete with its own bedroom. Meanwhile, Harper opted to demolish his little hut in favor of the larger one vacated by Doyle and Annie.

Always practical, Doyle initially suggested that Harper build his own quarters onto the new cabin, but Harper knew that because of Doyle's sense of propriety, he appreciated Harper's turning the offer down. Giving space to a married couple was noble, and although Harper wanted to believe this was the reason he refused better quarters, the reality was that he still believed he was unworthy of their love, of equal status, and of their home.

As the ranching operation grew, Doyle seemed more and more

uncomfortable with the other homesteads that began to populate the landscape. Many settlers came looking for silver, others for federal grazing lands, and still others for land claims. Most found less than they had hoped for. Even as Doyle disliked the company of anyone besides his friend and wife, Harper and Annie secretly enjoyed the perks offered by the growing town to the south. Harper for whiskey, tobacco, and other niceties; Annie for the mere pleasure of meeting other people.

She wasted no time on passersby or those in town who looked down on her—she identified them quickly enough—but she enjoyed conversation with anyone capable of being pleasant.

CHAPTER TWENTY

The Fall

Harper looked across the dimly lit saloon and locked eyes with the dusty, wiry man in the corner. Instantly, the message was clear to Harper.

You do not belong here, boy.

If Harper had been shrewd and nothing more, he might easily have dismissed the look, but Harper was also imaginative. This, along with his own self-hatred, amplified and distorted the man's true feelings into a different message.

You are traitors! You, your rebel friend ... and his Indian whore!

With one last look of disgust, the man placed his glass on the table, threw his coins down, and stalked out the door to the street.

Harper looked across the musty room to the barkeeper and lifted his finger, indicating he'd like another round.

"Who was that man, and why was he staring at me?" Harper asked as the whiskey poured.

"That would be Asa Stanley. He is a silver prospector ... successful, too, I believe—although I think a lot of that is exaggerated."

"What is his problem?"

He shrugged. "Could be because he thinks you are after his silver. He thinks everyone is."

"So, he glares at everyone like that?" Harper asked.

The barman shifted uncomfortably. "I suspect ... he has pegged you as a rebel. He fought for the Yankees in the war." He tilted his head. "Did he say something to you?"

Harper sniffed. "His look said it all."

Harper nursed his whiskey for an hour and nursed his grudge against Stanley until, without intending to, he rediscovered his mission of seeking justice for himself. Before long, their eyes would meet a second time, this time with Harper waiting in the dark with a drawn knife.

"Harper! Harper, where are you?"

Doyle sat up in his dream. His front was covered in blood, his back in frosty dew from the grass in which he lay. He crawled to Harper, who sat, catatonic, on the ground ten yards away.

"Harper, we have to go ... *now!*"

Doyle tugged at him. Without warning, Harper fell back, dead, blood softly seeping through the chest of his uniform.

Doyle's nightmares had been worsening; not that he ever said anything to Harper—or Annie, for that matter—but it was noticeable.

Harper noticed his friend's haggard appearance, his shortened temper, and his more-reclusive-than-usual behavior and knew exactly what it meant. He knew Doyle's history, knew what tortured him, and worst of all, recognized that Doyle was shutting him out. Whether or not Doyle's actions were intentional did not matter; all that mattered was that Doyle was rejecting his closest friend and upsetting the delicate balance of Harper's security.

Harper found himself deeply resentful, first of this situation and eventually of Doyle himself. Once again, Harper felt powerless. He did not know how to change the situation or how to protect Doyle. He began to wonder if Doyle was confiding in Annie. Did he trust his wife but not his oldest friend? Did he tell her that he didn't trust Harper? This idea rooted in Harper's mind—then there were two men lying awake each night.

Harper wanted nothing more than to give Doyle peace. He longed to convince Doyle that the incident on the battlefield was not what he thought. Harper had seen enough cowardice to know that being yellow was not an isolated action; rather, it was a character flaw existing in men who had no resolve. In his shame, Doyle had confused this character flaw with his own trauma, and only Harper held the knowledge and shared experience to free Doyle from this lie.

Harper, too, longed for the comfort that only truth could bring; to know that he was worth just as much as anyone else, that what people do and say—or don't—are almost always a reflection of themselves rather than those they hurt. Doyle was the only person from whom Harper could accept this truth. And so, while each man had the ability to carry the other, both remained blind to the help necessary to save their lives. Harper was certain Doyle would never listen to him or see the value of placing trust in others; Harper would never see the value in himself.

It was during these sleepless nights that Harper abandoned the idea of rest and attempted to busy himself in his hut. When this became no longer effective, he would quietly let himself outside to breathe in the night air. Finally, when this failed, he began roaming the countryside for hours on end. It invigorated him. Despite the influx of homesteaders, this was still an untamed country, and wandering in the dark presented just enough danger to make him feel alive.

Harper cautiously peered into the single window of the cabin. Tonight's roving had taken him farther than he'd wandered before—to a road just on the other side of which he spied a lighted cabin. His curiosity was instantly piqued. Something about the way it sat, juxtaposed to the road, reminded him of his childhood home. He tightened his grip on his walking stick and stole a look at the occupants.

A woman worked at something he could not quite make out. She reminded him of his own mother, although part of this could have been that the house had already reminded him of his old home. A small, wiry man sat working over what appeared to be a ledger of some sort. Harper clenched his teeth. It was Stanley. He strained his eyes for more details. He could just see a loft bed at the far end of the room that looked like it held two small children. They were the perfect picture of a pioneer household. Spartan, industrious, and complete, not unlike his own childhood. Of course, that had been before life had taught him that safety, security, and comfort were only a lingering myth so easily dispelled by tragedy and malice.

As he watched, he grew envious of the little family, jealous of a life that he wasn't sure existed. Was this a reality that he had missed out on? A quiet home with safe children, a mother at peace, and a father who would protect them? If it was true, Harper was resentful. If it was a lie, then they were frauds—and Harper hated them.

A low growl jerked Harper from his thoughts and froze his blood. Gathering his courage, he turned slowly to see the family mutt—teeth bared and hackles raised. Harper's grip tightened on his stick. There would be no secret way out of this. He could have called for the occupants to save him, made up a story about needing assistance, and developed an excuse for why he was traveling alone at night. Harper was capable of all this, but it wasn't to be. He imagined the family calling him a liar, accusing him, punishing him.

If his assumptions about the home made him angry, this newly imagined scenario made him furious. This so-called family, all the joy and opportunity that had eluded him in his twenty-seven years. Prejudice, defeatism, and unchecked rage boiled over until, without warning, he swung his stick, cleaving the dog's skull with a sickening crack. She let out a gasping whine, and her body twitched and scuffled on the ground. Harper scrambled from the cabin and dove behind a collection of barrels just as Asa Stanley burst through the door. He held a rifle in one hand, the lantern that lit the cabin in the other. His eyes swept the yard and landed on his dog's body.

"Worthless mutt," he growled. Harper watched as Asa cautiously approached the entrance to his little mine, looking, no doubt, for evidence of tampering. Stanley again turned his attention to the dog, bending down to inspect.

"Where are you?" he bellowed into the darkness. "Show yourselves!"

Harper stopped breathing. He was in deep trouble. He could see movement inside the cabin as Mrs. Stanley ran to ensure the children were protected. Asa again moved toward the mine entrance—the only thing that could provide cover to a trespasser.

Harper melted into the barrels that hid him from the angry, vengeful, self-righteous man. Stanley came closer. Harper pulled his knife and waited for the upper hand. Suddenly, Harper's blade glinted in the glow of the lantern, and Stanley stared directly at him. The instant their eyes met, Harper sprang, swinging his knife in an arc as he lunged. It was frantic and clumsy. Harper had overcommitted his weight and now had to recover his balance to strike again.

Less than a second later, prepared to bring the blade to Asa's chest, Harper saw the spray of blood from the man's neck. Stanley staggered back and dropped both gun and lantern, clutching the side of his throat. Somehow, Harper had landed a lethal wound in his initial swipe. Unwilling to take chances, he tackled Stanley to the ground to finish him. In a flash, he was back on top of Sergeant Johnson, on top of his stepfather, his mother, Wily Bill, Lloyd from the cattle drive, and everyone else who had ever wronged him. This worthless, judgmental fraud of a family man now became everyone and everything Harper hated, and suddenly there were not enough places for his knife. He drove the blade into Asa's chest again and again, transported to memories long forgotten: hateful children from his childhood; Ames, the storekeeper who always seemed to shake his head at Harper. Asa bore the wrath of everyone's sin.

Panicked screams pulled Harper's mind and body back together. Blood was everywhere, his hands, his legs, his face, eyes, and nose. Mrs. Stanley was in screaming hysterics. Everything between Asa's two arms was completely unrecognizable. Harper looked up at the woman in the doorway and saw his mother, standing in the home that he had been driven from so many years ago. Her children were crying inside, and she was frantically slamming the door. In a flash, Harper was at the door, kicking, pounding, cursing her—this selfish woman who pretended to love her children. With the family's only firearm lying next to Mr. Stanley, the bolted door was the family's last defense. Adrenaline pumping, Harper found a grip and roared as he pulled the door from its frame. He stood at the threshold, monstrous, dripping with sweat and blood, chest heaving with exertion, eyes full of rage, eyes that could neither be met nor averted, eyes that burned with the hatred of a thousand injustices, eyes that would never again see the light of reason.

CHAPTER TWENTY-ONE

Murder on the Frontier

TE NEXT MORNING WAS uncharacteristically cold, and Harper slept late to recover from the previous night's exhaustion.

Truthfully, it was a small miracle that Harper made it back to his hut undetected by the sleepless Doyle. William, the ranch's cow dog, knew Harper and did not bark when he returned. Harper had shed his torn, bloody clothes and stashed them under some boards that served as the floor to his hut. The whole night was a blur. He was aware of what he had done, but much of it seemed dream-like to him. By the time his fury had subsided, he was utterly exhausted. Still, he knew he had to do something to the crime scene to make suspicious eyes land elsewhere. It was an absolute mess, almost animal-like. No, worse than that. With little to work with, he had simply increased the carnage and devastation so that the attack would appear too brutal to even be human. He was satisfied, as he left the homestead, that once the scene was discovered there would be still more men on the frontier unable to sleep.

Over the next two days, Harper could tell that something was on Doyle's mind, and not knowing what it was unnerved him. He began to wonder if Doyle had seen him return in the early hours of the morning. The second day after the murder, Harper discovered the source of Doyle's moodiness.

"You hear the owl last night?" Doyle asked.

The question caught Harper off guard. Was Doyle speaking literally? There were no owls that he had heard or seen here. They both knew that owls carried a great deal of superstition anywhere, but none so much as in Annie's culture. Choctaw legend held that birds of the night represented death. Harper brushed the thoughts aside. Doyle didn't speak figuratively; if he suspected Harper of anything, he would ask point-blank—just as he had when he caught Harper in Captain Feral's haversack.

"No ... never in these parts."

"I suppose it could have nested in your hut and screamed all night without you knowing."

Harper gave a chuckle but didn't appreciate being reminded of the event from which the joke was derived. Being ridiculed and kicked because he didn't rouse quickly enough was what had prompted him to sabotage Feral's ammunition, which caused his death. Of course, Doyle didn't know all that and, therefore, could not appreciate the depth of Harper's resentment. Harper cleverly pointed out that Doyle never slept and, so, could not know if the owl was loud enough to wake anyone—if it was even real. Harper truly wondered if Doyle had really heard it or if his frayed nerves were toying with his mind.

He questioned Doyle, looking for clues. Had Annie heard it too? Was he sure he didn't simply imagine it? By the end of the conversation, Harper was convinced of two things: Doyle had heard the owl and did not suspect Harper of being anywhere but asleep in bed. What bothered Harper the most was that this otherwise insignificant event, albeit loaded with superstition, had transpired the same night as that of a very real evil. The idea that someone—something—supernatural might know what he had done made his skin crawl.

Harper hefted the axe for another swing. "Nothing good comes of owls."

The splintering of the last axe handle was enough for Doyle to call off all hopes of productivity and head into town. They already had a sizable list of necessities that had to be purchased, and today was as good as any.

Each man saddled a horse and began the trip to Weston. They rode in silence, Harper's mind whirring all the while. He was again lost, rejected by his friend, resentful toward his old family. He was justified in destroying the fake family, yet he might have gone too far this time.

No, it was not too far. It was right. They were evil, and they deserved to be exterminated—even the children. Nits make lice.

But then, what was this owl doing? Was it just an odd coincidence, or was it a harbinger of death? If it was a messenger, then who—or what—sent it?

Enough!

He needed to sort this out without driving himself mad. The idea occurred to Harper that he should lock himself in his hut every night for as long as it took to sort through his thoughts. This made him feel better, and before long, he had resolved to buy parchment and a pencil. He was a terrible writer, but that was okay. It would force him to go slowly and to organize his thoughts. His mind rested momentarily until he began to think about what he might hear once he and Doyle arrived in town.

There did indeed seem to be something hanging in the atmosphere in Weston. Once they had made their purchases, Harper excused himself for a drink while Doyle, who clearly had no interest in conversation, did whatever it was people do when they shut out everyone else. Harper was curious to find out if the mood in town was a reaction to the Stanley murders. Surely they had been discovered now that two days had passed—especially since the scene was visible all the way from the passing road.

Sure enough, from his vantage point in the saloon, Harper began to catch bits of conversations. The news had indeed arrived but only about an hour before he and Doyle. He was careful to be inconspicuous as he listened to the men pass details about the discovery.

"It was Lincoln who found it," one man said.

"Maybe it was Lincoln what done it," replied another, beer dribbling down his red beard.

"The sheriff's cousin tore four people to pieces, George?" the first man asked.

George grunted.

"I do not care if he is the pope's cousin. Sitting next to the law does not make you righteous."

Harper's ears perked up. George's disdain for those in power resonated with him. He liked George.

"It was Injuns, plain and simple, fellas," said a third man. "If Lincoln could tell from the road something was amiss, then that is all I need to know."

The first man continued.

"Well, as I said, Lincoln's boys said they seen Asa from the road. Lincoln drew his gun, took one look inside the house, and sent his boys to Weston at a full gallop for Schutz."

"As they drove out of sight, the youngest boy saw his daddy doubled over vomiting," said the third man."

"You think old Stanley cheated the Indians?" the first man said.

"Why not?" George asked. "He was a prospector, after all. I guess we will find out when they compare his ledger to his silver—if there is anything left after everyone ransacks his home."

The third man spoke again. "Asa was no sweetie, but was no crook, either."

Harper busied himself with his whiskey. So far, it didn't sound like there were any suspects—besides the natives. He ordered another drink, and noticed the man on his right was watching him. He ignored the patron, keeping his ears up for more information.

After watching a minute or two longer, the man slid closer to Harper. "You know Sutton?"

No introduction, just the question—and it instantly irritated Harper. Who was this drunk, and what did he want?

"Why are you asking?" Harper replied.

"He is your neighbor. You are the Rebel Ranch, are you not? With the Indian woman?"

Harper tensed. Was he looking for a fight? Was he going to turn everyone in the saloon against him? Harper's anger began to rise. He could crush this man, only he'd never do it because of the backlash against himself, Doyle, and Annie that would surely follow. Hiding his powerlessness, he turned slowly toward the other man and stared him down.

"Yes. I fought for the rebels. Yes. I am on a ranch with the Indian. Yes. Sutton is the closest homestead to me." He leaned in to the man. "What do you want?"

The man looked intensely at Harper for several moments and then burst out with a loud laugh that reeked of beer.

Stupid sot.

"I knew it was yooou ..." he slurred. "I just wanted to know if you know Sutton. If you know him ... for what he really is."

Harper watched the man drain his beer.

"He is a cheat ... and a hypocrite! Always talking about God and goodness but withholding the wages of those he exploits!"

The waning of Harper's patience abated. This interested him. Yet another story of a man who pretended to be something he was not. It was so familiar—so infuriatingly familiar—to him.

"What are you talking about?" Harper nudged, unable to help himself.

"He has more wealth than anyone, but it is ill-gotten. I worked a week for the man, and he refuses to pay."

Now, righteous indignation rose within Harper. He didn't know Mr. Sutton, but if he was wealthy, then, as far as Harper was concerned, it was only because he took advantage of others. That was the way things worked.

Harper's drinking partner leaned in close. "I hope the Indians kill him next."

"Of course, Indians," Harper muttered to himself. "Who else would they blame?"

"Huh?" said the drunk.

Harper ignored him. It hadn't been his intent to cast suspicion on the indigenous tribes, and even though it cleared him as a suspect, the rashness of the good people of Weston was irritating to him. Harper had been the scapegoat enough to recognize when blame was cast unfairly.

Anywhere but themselves.

An equally rash thought flickered across his consciousness. He should kill every last one of these devils and send them to hell where they belonged.

The drunk looked at him sideways. "What did you say?"

Harper threw back his drink, slammed the glass on the counter, and walked out. Outside, he saw Doyle about twenty paces away, apparently wrapping up a conversation with a man. It was a preacher. What was Doyle doing with a preacher? They even seemed friendly. What was going on with him?

He will not talk to me, but he will have a nice chat with a preacher? Unbelievable.

Once the minister bade farewell to Doyle and crossed the street,

Harper approached Doyle and touched his shoulder.

"You ready? This place is making me uneasy."

CHAPTER TWENTY-TWO

THE ORDER OF THE ISHKITINI

FOR THE NEXT THREE nights, Harper journaled feverishly—if it could be called journaling. It was no manifesto; it was a tangled mess of thoughts, ideas, and memories spilling over the pages:

hatefull

rong

wickid

Disorganized as it was, he found it soothing. Writing for hours, reading, rereading, and filling in the gaps allowed Harper to sort through the labyrinth that his mind had become. For the first time, someone was paying attention—he was listening to himself now. The more his ideas and thoughts went unchallenged, the more the deepest desires of his heart began to make sense.

if only you wuld slay the wickid ...

venjense is mine

owl ... Ishkateeny ... O-foon-low

The little screech owl, what Annie called Ofunlo, had proclaimed that Harper was ordained to the order of Ishkitini. Instead of accepting evil, he exacted justice, even when no one else would. For this reason, Ofunlo had cried, as best Harper could determine, at the exact moment he had killed Stanley. Ishkitini was no witch, no murderer. He was a righteous angel sent to destroy evildoers. Harper had suffered at the hands of those who went unpunished, had failed to accept the injustice, and now something—fate, maybe—had appointed him to become Ishkitini, to restore the moral balance of the universe. His actions were validated and deemed righteous. Accepting his calling now authorized Harper to take his hurt out on the world that had so abused him.

I will slay the wickid

By day, Harper held his peace, completing chores, ranging cattle, cutting firewood—even as Doyle became more distant. By night, he gave his full attention to becoming Ishkitini.

With nothing to inform him besides what he could remember of Annie's descriptions, he meticulously crafted his ceremonial getup, taking complete artistic license in carving a cruel beak and affixing black roping locks onto the headdress. He fashioned long metal claws that could be wielded in an initial attack, yet which he could quickly shed when he needed more dexterity. It took him over a week to finish, overlaying the entire thing with an assortment of feathers. He worked insatiably, building up his religion, covering every twinge of doubt with claws and feathers. The costume was impressive and terrifying, and the more awesome it became, the more Harper worshipped what he had become until, finally, the last vestiges of truth were completely banished from his conscience.

He was Ishkitini.

A few nights later, Harper crept out of his hut, holding his alter ego in his arms. William stirred from his spot on the Hills' porch and trotted over to inspect. He sniffed the costume eagerly and began to wag after Harper as he walked off the property.

"Go home!" Harper hissed.

The dog balked, then started back after Harper as soon as his back was turned.

"*Go!*" Harper repeated, kicking at him to show he meant business.

William dropped his tail and headed back to the cabin. Harper made his way across the road and donned his gear. Next stop would be the Sutton homestead, where they would learn too late the deadly consequences of cheating those less fortunate than themselves.

Sutton was the closest homestead to what the locals apparently referred to as Rebel Ranch—a name none of them liked, particularly Annie—and it didn't take long for Harper to arrive. Seeing nothing from the window and finding the door secured, Harper took a pause. It was a solid door, and Harper did not dare use force against it without knowing exactly where Mr. Sutton and his guns lay.

Just like a guilty man to lock himself up like this.

He needed a better plan. Sutton would live tonight, but his day would come.

Discontented, Harper set out for the next homestead. He thought he remembered who lived there, and, if memory served well, he hadn't liked these settlers much more than he'd liked Asa Stanley. He'd seen how they watched him from the road as they passed the so-called Rebel Ranch. His disappointment in his inability to dispatch Sutton worked hard to justify his changed plan, and his bloodlust was rewarded when he quietly found a way inside the second home and tore the family to pieces in the dark.

Harper now had a purpose that he understood, and this better prepared him to think through his actions. After arranging the crime scene so grotesquely that no one could reasonably call it the work of human hands, Harper made it home to his hut, shed his garments, and safely hid the costume before day broke. In contrast to his first two murders, he was no longer overcome by emotion; he was a man on a mission, and his improved efficiency was a sign to him that he was doing what was right.

Hearing people discuss his first massacre in the saloon two weeks prior had racked Harper's nerves, but the news heralded by the dispatched riders the day after his second attack was exhilarating. Despite becoming nervous when he found out that he had left a survivor—a young girl who had slid into a crawl space as Harper had ripped into her father—he was also filled with awe at the description of the demon who'd killed the girl's family. Harper was now more convinced than ever that he was finally experiencing the purpose of his life.

Even the fear on Annie's face could not bring him down. The only thing that deprived him of his high spirits was Doyle's increased moodiness, which again reminded him that he had been shut out.

That night, as he scribbled his notes, he pondered what to do about Doyle:

duz Doyle care about me

worth-less

test Doyle

Was he still of value to Doyle—after all they had been through together? Doyle would never approve of his new life purpose, but did Doyle even care to stick by him as a friend? He had to know. He would put Doyle to the test the next chance he got.

The opportunity to speak privately with Doyle came the next afternoon as he, Harper, and Annie ranged their little herd. It would be one of the last good opportunities for the cattle to graze before what little vegetation was left went dormant. Doyle was in a daze, sitting motionless in the saddle as Harper approached him.

"You all right there, boss?" Harper forced himself to sound good-natured.

"Jeez, Rod!" Doyle started.

He must be really out of it. It wasn't like Harper had snuck up on him.

Harper pretended to remain upbeat. He didn't want Doyle to think anything was amiss, but he didn't have a whole lot of patience left, either. He decided to cut to the chase.

"How long are we staying, Hill?"

It was a fair question, and not entirely out of the blue either. Doyle knew that life was no better here than anywhere else and that, besides Doyle and Annie being here, Harper had no ties to the place. None of them had moved out here to start a desert ranch, and there was no reason they couldn't pull stakes and settle elsewhere.

Harper also knew Doyle's position. He was tired. This place

wasn't perfect, but, despite the increase in population, it was still open and quiet. As far as the Hills were concerned, this was good enough, and so long as they had each other, it was as good a place as any. Harper, on the other hand, was younger and less tired. Why not find a better place together?

"Where would you have me go, Rod?"

Harper thought he detected more exasperation than curiosity. "Texas."

Of course Texas, always Texas. They were both from Texas. It was country they knew well, and the same effort they applied here would give them ten times the reward there. Additionally, their neighbors wouldn't see them as traitors.

"I will stay, Rod," Doyle said quietly. "You may stay or go ..."

There it was. Doyle clearly didn't value his opinion. He didn't even seem to care about him. Harper made one last attempt to see if Doyle cared whether his closest friend stayed or left.

"I may go."

Doyle looked at Harper, who stared straight back, waiting for a response.

"You know they will find it—him. They will find him and kill him."

What kind of a response is that?

It was no answer, it was a change of subject. Harper burned inside. Doyle was fast losing his sainthood.

"Maybe the demon is a sign." Harper felt some satisfaction in giving an undetectable warning.

His calling to the order of Ishkitini had gifted him with the ability to hide his emotions better than Doyle. He had become more cunning than Wily Bill, more ruthless than Sergeant Johnson, and more distant than his family. He was now the ruler of his destiny and more powerful than he'd ever thought possible.

It was time to make a sacrifice, and he decided to try the Sutton homestead again. If he could get underneath the floor of the home, he might find enough loose boards to let himself in without losing the element of surprise.

CHAPTER TWENTY-THREE

Hunted

THAT NIGHT, EMBOLDENED IN his righteous purpose, Harper became Ishkitini in his hut and stole into the night toward his target. He had made his way halfway to the property line when William rushed him, barking madly at what he apparently judged to be an intruder.

Harper remembered how quickly things had unraveled at Stanley's mine after their dog had discovered him. In one swift motion, Harper grabbed William by the neck. The dog thrashed violently, trying to bite the demon. Harper threw him against the tree to avoid his teeth, knocking William unconscious. Harper was furious. His plans had been ruined; his divine appointment interrupted. In his anger, he unleashed his wrath on poor William the same way he had on Asa only two weeks before.

Suddenly, Harper was aware of a voice. Doyle was calling William's name. Harper jerked his head toward the cabin. In the dim moonlight, the two men beheld each other. Harper could just make out the outline of Doyle's rifle. Hoping Doyle would retreat, Harper stood up, slowly, menacingly, every movement deliberately planned to put fear into the other man.

He whispered to himself, "Go back inside, Doyle."

He had to scare Doyle back into the cabin. It was the only way he'd be able to double back and sneak into bed without being found out. He would have to sort the rest out in the morning after pretending to have slept through the ordeal.

He flexed his claws, hoping Doyle could see them, and twisted his head to the side, mimicking the motion of an owl.

Without warning, Doyle sprinted toward him. Harper made a dash for the dry creek bed on the edge of the ranch; it was the closest feature in the landscape that would provide cover if Doyle started shooting.

Quickly reaching the safety of the gully, Harper threw his shoulders back and split the night with his own unearthly screech. Maybe it would rattle Doyle and throw him off the pursuit. He moved cautiously through the gully, keeping watch for Doyle and hoping he had given up the chase. He was again startled by the sight of Doyle, who was now moving along the bank. Harper worked to keep his wits. He couldn't panic and flee, or he might be shot; he had to play a longer game.

Minutes dragged by, and Harper's fear gave way to annoyance. Why was it that the brooding, distant Doyle had somehow found courage only when it suited Harper the least? Now, instead of completing his ordained mission, he was being hunted by someone he least expected.

Each time he attempted to double back and return home, Doyle caught sight of him and renewed the chase, forcing Harper to move farther down the creek bed. He was running out of options. Unable to think of anything better, he decided to shed his gear and become Harper again. Maybe he could convince Doyle that he'd awoken and come to investigate.

Taking advantage of the quiet, he peeled off the costume and stashed it—as best he could—in the scraggly brush at the edge of the gully. It was a convenient hiding place, not good, but convenient. Once he joined Doyle as Harper again, he would steer him away from the spot. He crouched, waiting for an opportunity to make his appearance. Doyle appeared, silhouetted against the moon. Harper could tell from his stance that he was searching. Both men watched and waited with bated breath, far longer than was comfortable; Doyle looking for Harper, Harper watching Doyle. At last, Doyle's posture relaxed. He was done; Harper had won the game. He waited for Doyle to head home, mentally charting the best path to his own hut. He'd have to grab his costume and find a better place for it as Doyle would be back looking for clues at first light. If he could, Harper would also need to dispose of William. The kill was sloppy, and he wasn't sure that Doyle would buy into a completely inhuman attacker once he inspected the body.

Harper watched Doyle turn and begin to pick his way between the edge of the bank and the scrub growth that crowded against the creek bed. Without warning, a screech erupted, followed by a furious flapping of wings. Doyle was knocked backward and fell into the creek bed. It was the break Harper needed, and he streaked toward his hut.

Harper arrived breathless and, casting a quick look in the direction of the cabin, ducked inside his hut, panting heavily. He had to gather himself, calm down, and develop a plan. He *had* to retrieve the costume, no matter what. The dog's body was beyond his control.

As his mind processed the events of the evening, it occurred to him that the screech he'd heard before Doyle fell had to have come from another owl. It must have been huge to knock Doyle into the creek bed. It made sense, though, since Harper was ordained, that the bird had been sent to deliver him, to preserve his purpose and further his mission. *It was exhilarating! Surely, here was proof that—*

His thoughts were cut short as the door, which he had failed to bolt, was violently yanked open.

Certain it was Doyle, Harper threw himself on his bed, pretending to sleep. All at once, Annie was on top of him, crying, pulling him from his bed.

"What? What is it?" he said with mock grogginess.

"Wake up! Get up! Get your gun!"

Harper grabbed her by the shoulders. "Annie ... *Annie!* Stop!"

She breathed in deeply and blinked her eyes hard. "He is out there with ... something ... I do not know, but ... I think it has got him!"

Harper took her head in his hands and looked straight at her. "Go to the cabin. Get a light. Meet me outside."

She nodded, and Harper followed her out, rifle in hand. He

wasn't sure how this would play out, but he needed to find Doyle, hand him over to his wife, and pledge to continue the search so that he could retrieve Ishkitini.

Annie joined him in the yard, and Harper began to occupy her with questions.

"Annie, what have you seen?"

"Doyle heard, and he ... he rushed out the door!"

"You saw nothing? What did Doyle see?"

Annie said nothing but continued to look around frantically.

Harper stood in front of her. "Annie, listen to me. What did Doyle see?"

"Nothing, nothing! It was what we heard! An ow—it was the Ishkitini! Doyle went after him and ... and ... and ..."

"Follow me, we will find him."

As quickly as possible, Harper led Annie toward the creek, carefully skirting the grove where William lay. The sooner they found Doyle, the better. Harper wasn't aware of any owl calls prior to the shriek he'd let out. Had he been so occupied in dispatching William that he had missed it? He needed to be more careful. It did comfort him, however, that Annie seemed to know nothing more. She, of course, was convinced that Ishkitini was real and that he was here—Harper knew this without asking. He also knew that Doyle put no stock in such things, and it puzzled him that Doyle had even bothered to investigate. Harper had dismissed Doyle's claim that he would shoot the next owl he saw—it wasn't really the type of thing a practical man like Doyle would do—but perhaps he was determined to show Annie that it was just a bird.

Annie began calling Doyle's name, and Harper joined in. The last thing he needed was for Doyle to think the monster had returned and then start shooting at them. He led Annie to the place he had last seen Doyle. She gasped at his prone body in the dried bed, and they both rushed to his side. He was breathing but unconscious.

"I think he fell, Annie," Harper said deductively, holding the lantern on the scuff marks where Doyle had last stood. "I do not know what he was doing, but it does not look like foul play."

His words calmed Annie a little, and she turned her full attention to her husband. Doyle stirred, and Harper helped him to sit up as he roused. Harper needed to find out what he remembered, what conclusions he had come to, and what he would do next. Annie had her own questions, and between the two of them, they overwhelmed poor Doyle. Eventually, Harper gave up his quest for information and addressed Annie. "There is nothing here, but I will continue to look for a bit."

Doyle stood up, and Harper went to help him. Doyle waved him off. Typical Doyle.

Harper backed away from the couple. "Annie, help him back to the cabin—and make him rest."

The sky was beginning to lighten as Harper ran to recover his gear. Annie and Doyle were inside their home, and Harper was able to safely stow his disguise under the boards of his hut with his journals. He then returned to the grove of trees where William lay and quickly buried the body. Once he found what Doyle knew, he'd explain that he'd found the dog and disposed of him. Finally, he went to the cabin to find out what he could.

Annie had propped Doyle up on the bed. He looked undignified and irritable, and Harper knew he likely didn't have much patience left in him. Once Annie was out of earshot, Harper approached Doyle cautiously and told him what Annie had told him about Ishkitini. When Doyle didn't bite, Harper went straight in.

"What did you see out there?"

Doyle blanched but quickly countered, "Who says there was anything besides an owl?"

Harper was disgusted. It was all the validation he needed to know that Doyle had no intention of including him. He had shut Harper out completely.

"I found the dog," Harper said flatly, enjoying the look of surprise on Doyle's face. He then heaped an appropriate amount of guilt on Doyle by explaining that he had hidden William to protect Annie's nerves.

"There is something out there, Rod." Doyle eventually confessed. "I do not know what."

Maybe there is some hope for Doyle. It had clearly taken a lot for him to give just a little ground, but perhaps Doyle would finally bring him up to speed and enlist his help in hunting Ishkitini. Harper wanted this—and didn't want it. He didn't fully understand it, but even though Doyle's confidence in him would mean putting his mission on hold indefinitely, it would be a worthy sacrifice to know that Doyle—that anyone—valued him.

CHAPTER TWENTY-FOUR

Town in a Panic

Doyle's spirits seemed to rise over the next two days, but Harper's disappointment in his friend's continued reticence soon returned. He again found himself pacing his hut in frustration until finally deciding that Ishkitini needed to come alive again.

Sutton still needed to be held accountable for his crimes, but for now, he would have to wait. There was plenty of justice to mete out, and Ishkitini demanded quicker justice. To put it another way, Harper needed quicker gratification. He remembered how the drunkard had been quick to blame Native Americans for the Stanley murders and recalled that everyone seemed to think that way. He remembered how, at that moment, he had recognized that every last one of those fools stood convicted in his mind.

That night, in full regalia, he stood outside a little cabin and peered at the nursing mother inside.

News of Ishkitini's latest attack traveled quickly. The town was in an uproar over the killings, and assistance from the US Army had been requested. Doyle was uncharacteristically intent on attending the meeting at the courthouse. Harper suspected he was seeking information that could be of use to him, information for which Doyle needed to look no further than his alienated friend.

"Doyle, why do you want to attend this meeting?" Harper asked. "It is not like you."

"I want to know what people think."

"What do *you* think, Doyle?"

"I do not know what I think."

Harper knew better. Doyle at least had an *idea* of what he was looking for. After all, he had chased the Ishkitini through the night. It was clear that Doyle was trying to solve the mystery on his own, and it was approaching the point where it threatened more than just their friendship. If Doyle didn't stop, it would threaten Harper's very purpose.

The courthouse meeting the following day confirmed Harper's judgment against the townspeople. Indians, Indians, and Indians were all people could talk about. Savages coming for their families. Harper felt that if he was ever caught, the mob would simply assume he had been working on behalf of Indians. The public's prejudice both protected Harper and condemned them in his mind.

Outside the courthouse, Doyle looked up at the sky. "Nasty weather coming—and it will be dark by the time it passes. I will arrange for us to board here tonight."

Harper's mood turned nasty right along with the weather. He was growing dubious of anyone's ability to stand blameless, and the events that night would soon remove all doubt from his mind.

Harper lay sleepless in the stable behind the store where Doyle and Annie had lodged. He stared up at the timbers, pondering the utter depravity of men. He had found meaning in exterminating evil, but it now seemed futile. Everyone was evil. Even Doyle, and by extension, Annie. Was he supposed to kill everyone? Everyone but himself? Suddenly, the words Doyle had spoken to him years ago, by the latrine in the camp during the war, bubbled to the surface of his consciousness.

"Who can stand, Rod?"

Harper heard footsteps approaching. His thoughts suddenly turned to grabbing whoever was outside, pulling them into his stable, and putting an end to them. It was a fine fantasy. It felt good, but Harper was aware that it no longer carried with it a sense of purpose. The footsteps stopped outside the stable, and someone let themselves in. It was likely John, the store owner, coming to check on his guest.

Harper pretended to sleep until the receding footsteps told him the intruder was gone. He kept his eyes closed and fumed for what felt like hours. Even a scream from the distant street barely registered. Why shouldn't there be suffering and evil here? People were evil, so where people were, evil was sure to follow—even when they gathered for safety.

More footsteps. Lighter, hurried ones sounded into the stable. Harper began his act of sleeping again and refused to stir until he was shaken.

Annie ... again.

"What, woman?" he asked, hiding the true source of his frustration in feigned weariness.

"There is something going on in the street outside, and I cannot find Doyle."

Good. Let Doyle go off alone and play the hero. Maybe he just wants to escape your never-ending fretting!

Of course, Harper would never say this. He was measured—self-controlled—in everything but bloodlust. He rose and pulled on his boots. "Let us find him ... again."

They found Doyle in front of the saloon, and not a moment too soon. His knifepoint was pushed into Thacker's neck—Thacker, the man who had never learned to shut his mouth. Harper stared as Annie walked right up to the men and defused the entire situation with a single touch on Doyle's arm. Even Harper had to admit that it was remarkable.

Two men took the woman's body away, and the sheriff's deputies arrested a young man—a railroader—for her murder; a white man, like everyone else in the street that night. Harper heard a comment that the railroad was bringing nothing but criminals.

These fools will point their fingers at anything that moves.

Annie and Harper had witnessed the same fear in the crowd. In those moments, Annie had used her ability to ease their suffering, to save a man's life, and to redeem her husband from certain ruin. Whether or not Annie realized it, she had just calmed the crowd, which gradually dispersed.

Harper, by contrast, was responsible for their fear, and in those moments, he fully resigned himself. Mankind—everyone—was worthless. Justice had always been futile. What difference could justice make if no one could stand?

Harper did not sleep for the next three nights. All was lost. He had again lost his purpose and his place in the world. His mind wandered throughout the realm of imagination, just as he himself had wandered throughout his life: without meaning, belonging, or peace. The only thoughts that brought him a measure of satisfaction were the memories of killing those who had hurt him, the fantasy of killing others who had wronged him, and the feeling of killing them again and again through surrogates. He dumped his thoughts out on paper.

meaning-less
meaning-less
meaning-less

There was no longer any energy to sort through them. Nevertheless, as he wrote, his focus narrowed, and his mind began to align emotion and logic until finally, he arrived at the conclusion that had eluded him for so long.

worth-less
I am worth-less
they are worth-less
every-thing is meaning-less

He *was* worthless, but so was everyone else. Nothing mattered except that which felt good. He had wasted years justifying that which felt good, making it morally acceptable—necessary, even.

Suddenly, he understood that he had never needed a reason. Ishkitini was not an agent of divine appointment. He was a witch, a monster. He was Harper, and Harper could no longer justify murder, nor did he care to. It was simply something—the only thing—that brought him peace.

After pulling out Ishkitini from underneath the floorboards, Harper replaced it with his scribblings. He dressed slowly, methodically, cherishing the anticipation. He relished the feeling of power growing within him as he donned the headdress and claws. *This* is what made him feel alive. Killing. Fulfilling his desire. He would never again suppress it. He was who he was, and for the first time, he embraced it.

Calmly, he opened the door and left his hut. Looking at the cabin across the way, he let his muscles ripple. He had fully become Ishkitini. He had become death.

PART III

REDEMPTION

IF I GO UP TO THE HEAVENS, YOU ARE THERE; IF I MAKE MY BED IN THE DEPTHS, YOU ARE THERE. IF I RISE ON THE WINGS OF THE DAWN, IF I SETTLE ON THE FAR SIDE OF THE SEA, EVEN THERE YOUR HAND WILL GUIDE ME.

PSALM 139:8–10

CHAPTER TWENTY-FIVE

Vigilantes

Henry Schutz bid the jailer good night and stepped into the street. He lit a cigarette and stood outside for several minutes, clearing his mind before the walk home. This had become his custom on hard days. Step outside, smoke, and mentally peel off the sheriff badge.

Life had changed so much in five years, and most days now seemed hard. Weston had always been a little rough, but now it was a city, a city that required regulations, formalities, and so on. The railroad had made a lot of people rich, but, so far, all it had done for Henry was make him tired.

Henry enforced law and order. Weston had always been rough; but since the small town had become a city, "rough" was unacceptable. Henry was a committed lawman but no politician. If things didn't improve, the railroad would replace him with their own. They wouldn't be employees of the Central Pacific, of course, but they would be owned by the company one way or another. They would be burdened with this conflict of interest, and it would be evident in the way they executed their duties.

"We will have a word, Sheriff."

Schutz looked up to see four men approaching him out of the dark. Two of them, brothers from the Alder family—one of the first families to settle these parts—he recognized. The other two, he did not know.

He suspected he knew what this was about, and it was not good.

"Shoot," Henry replied, his response both an invitation and a dare.

The elder Alder, Frederick, spoke. "We have come for your prisoner."

"Oh?" Henry asked.

"We will hold trial," Alder continued, "and execution when found guilty. You need not concern yourself with this matter."

Schutz adjusted his hat and pretended to consider the virtues of Alder's demands before responding.

"Well, gentlemen," he began, "as duly appointed sheriff, I must concern myself in all matters of the law. You and I cannot pick and choose who will execute justice in this or that."

"Look, Shoots," the younger Alder butted in, pronouncing the sheriff's surname with the pun—and skill—for which Henry was known. "There are things which you see to, and there are things, such as this, which require ..." he searched, "other ... measures."

"Other measures?" Henry asked. "You have already condemned the accused, Charlie, so you may as well just call it a lynching."

The men adopted a more threatening stance, but Henry wasn't

finished. This had to be put to rest now before the group returned as a mob. He addressed Frederick directly.

"The days of vigilance committees are gone, son. Justice will be served. I will see this through."

Frederick squared his shoulders but did not advance.

"If you stand in the way of justice, Sheriff, you will be replaced."

Henry knew Frederick wasn't talking about reelection, but he pretended to miss the threat.

"Oh, I expect that will happen soon enough, Fred ... the rail company will see to that."

Fred's face darkened. "Hand over the prisoner." His tone was even.

Henry had been here before. It wasn't the first time he'd reached the end of negotiations with men who couldn't be reasoned with. The abandonment of reason in favor of what they desired, claiming things like justice and righteousness to suit their needs, no, this was nothing new—and neither was the next step. He put his hands on his hips.

"Gentlemen," he began in a businesslike tone. "I cannot resolve this to your satisfaction, so it comes down to this: I will die tonight, if necessary, to preserve justice—true justice." He rested the heel of his right hand on the handle of his holstered revolver. "The question that remains," he continued, "is who among you will die first to preserve blind vengeance?"

The last two words departed from the conversational tone Henry had maintained throughout the ordeal. Their echo in the street told the vigilantes that there was no more discussion to be had.

Sheriff Schutz looked each man in the eye, starting with the two tagalongs, then Charlie. By the time he stared into Fred's eyes, he knew it was over. Fred wouldn't act alone, and he had seen that none of the others were willing to make a move. He was defeated.

"We will speak on this again, Sheriff," said Fred without much conviction. Then, to his crew, he said, "Come on, boys, let him see what 'justice' he can find for us."

CHAPTER TWENTY-SIX

Condemned

A THIN MAN WALKED through the jailhouse door, flooding the little building with sunlight and illuminating the dust in the air. The door closed behind him, and everything went dim and stuffy again. He removed his hat and cleared his throat, unnecessarily announcing his presence to the man behind the single desk. He was tall and appeared uncomfortable as he ducked slightly under the beams of the low ceiling.

The room's inhabitant looked up from his chair and grimaced, put out at having to interrupt his card-play for the visitor.

"Mr. Carson," he said, turning his attention back to his cards.

"Mr. James," Carson returned. He rolled his eyes at James's purposeful dullness, then gestured with his hat toward the figure that occupied the little cell on the back wall.

"This is the accused?" Carson failed to hide the doubt in his voice.

"That is the *killer*," James replied without looking up. "I expect you want to speak with your client before trial?"

"That is how this is done, yes," Carson said, dismissing the reference to the accused as his client. He was annoyed. Every time he and the circuit judge showed up, he had to have this conversation. It would be nice if the sheriff would deputize competent lawmen and leave his relatives to clean stables as they didn't seem capable of much else.

James clearly found more gratification in ignoring Carson's tone than in responding in kind. He likely figured the sooner this conversation ended, the better.

"I will leave you to it, then," he said, gathering up his deck. He stood up and retrieved his hat from the hook on the wall.

"If you've read the charges, you'll keep your distance." James paused at the door, his hand on the knob. "It will not take long; it is an open-and-shut case, and the murderer has not said a word." James opened the door to the busy street and, as an afterthought, announced loudly, "I will have the gallows ready tomorrow."

The door banged shut. Carson regarded the caged figure carefully and chewed his lip. Ignoring James's warning, he grabbed the chair, sat directly in front of the cell's bars, and addressed the occupant. "Mrs. Hill?"

Silence.

"Mrs. Hill, my name is Daniel Carson. I will be attending your arraignment tomorrow with Judge Griffiths, who has appointed me to investigate this matter."

She stared up at him, and Carson got his first good look at the shell of a woman before him, wasting away from malnutrition and, he didn't know, maybe a broken heart.

"Mrs. Hill, you have been accused of twelve murders. Twelve senseless, brutal murders that, from what I hear, could not have been committed by someone of your size ..."

Annie shifted her gaze and said nothing.

"There is more to this than what I have been told, is there not, Annie?"

She looked back at Carson as though hearing her name for the first time.

Carson continued. "But only you can set it straight."

Annie sat, still and silent, refusing to defend herself. Carson had seen this type of behavior before. He had read the case report. She was alone, with no one left on earth whom she loved. In one awful night, she had become accused by all and loved by none. She was ready to die.

After several minutes, Carson finally pulled his chair back to the desk and donned his hat. He looked at Annie and sighed.

"I suspect you should not hang for these crimes, Annie, but I cannot help you if you will not help yourself. If you decide to speak—" he jerked his head toward the empty desk, "have the fat one send for me."

Privately degrading James was his last bid to gain some ground with Annie—there was no way she didn't hate him. When she refused to react, he walked to the door and lifted the latch.

"Goodbye, Mrs. Hill."

Carson walked down the street toward the hotel. The whole situation was rotten. There was no way this woman was anything more than a scapegoat, but without a defense, she'd be no better off than if the old vigilante committees still ran things. The state justice system had improved drastically over the years, but he doubted it would make a difference to Annie. Was she refusing to speak, or was she simply too damaged?

He nearly bumped into a man who had been trying to get his attention and was startled from his thoughts.

"Good afternoon," the man said. "Are you representing Mrs. Hill tomorrow?"

"Daniel Carson," he said. "Mrs. Hill has no defense counsel. However, I have been appointed to represent the people." He paused, considering the ramifications of his next sentence. "Although, in this case, I think that includes Mrs. Hill."

He wasn't sure if he was about to be scolded, punched, or hammered with questions, but he suspected something bad. Settlers had been murdered, an Indian was in prison, and, as most people saw it, he was part of a system that stood in the way of justice.

The man offered his hand. "Samuel ... Sutton. We need to talk."

CHAPTER TWENTY-SEVEN

One Last Breath

Early Winter 1873

Harper's claws drove deep into Doyle's throat. He sputtered and gurgled; his eyes glazed over. Suddenly, Harper heard Annie's voice calling for Doyle from the house. He jerked his head toward the sound and pricked up his ears. She was getting closer. It was her time now.

Suddenly, Doyle came to life, grabbing Harper's feathered arms and staring directly into his eyes.

Harper leaned in to Doyle's ear. "Do not worry, my friend. I will make sure she is with you soon—no one will suspect her."

Doyle's grip loosened, and his hand fell lifeless at his side. It was now Annie's turn.

On the other side of the rocks, Annie peered into the darkness.

"Doyle!" she screamed. "*Doyle!*"

The owl's call—taunting, cruel, evil—stopped Annie in her tracks. She heard rustling behind the boulder to her left. A grisly figure barreled around into her full view. The night was dark, and though the details were difficult to make out, it was Ishkitini ... but without a beak. She knew he was coming for her, and she knew she would die tonight.

What she had done to meet such an end, she did not know, but in that instant, it did not matter. She could not fight against the creature of the night and win, but for now, she was still alive, still human, and her human mind told her she had to try to survive, however futile it seemed.

She swung her hands up and squeezed her husband's revolver hard. She neither heard the shot nor felt the pistol snap her wrists upward. She squeezed it again. Again. Again. The figure was on the ground, kicking in spasms, dying, then motionless. Click, click, click, click, click.

"*Doyle!*" Annie screamed.

She dropped to her knees, panting heavy puffs of fog into the air. The owl called again from above, and she fainted.

CHAPTER TWENTY-EIGHT

THE TRIAL

ANNIE SAT IN THE little courtroom. She was there in body only. Besides her, there was Judge Griffiths, the sheriff; Carson, the district attorney; two other lawmen; and her neighbor, Sam Sutton. Annie's mind had wasted away in her body. Her body had wasted away in her little cell. Over a month had passed between the night she lost everything and the day the circuit judge finally made his way back to Weston to hear the case against her.

Preliminary procedures were dealt with in a perfunctory manner, and Judge Griffiths read the charges.

"Annie Hill, you stand accused of the murder of Rodney Harper, Doyle Hill, Asa Stanley ..."

The list went on. By the time Griffiths was finished, he had named twelve souls.

Deputy Candon introduced the others.

"Counsel for the state of Nevada, fifth circuit, Mr. Daniel Carson. Special witnesses, Sheriff Henry Schutz, Samuel Sutton ..."

Annie stared straight ahead. She was ready for this parliamentary abomination of justice to end so that she could face the gallows.

"Mrs. Hill!" Griffiths was bellowing at her. "Mrs. Hill, do you understand the charges against you? Do you speak English?" He turned to Schutz. "Does she speak English?"

Annie's mind flashed back eight years to when Doyle had asked her the same question. A tear escaped and ran down her face.

"Your Honor," Carson said. "If I may, neighbors have provided testimony that the defendant has adequate command of the English language, and deputies have stated that Mrs. Hill has not spoken since her arrest. Mr. Sutton, here, testifies she has not spoken since he found her, half frozen, on her property six weeks ago, Tuesday."

Griffiths eyed her, then, addressing Carson, said, "How does she plead?"

"Not guilty, Your Honor."

"She told you this?"

"Not as such, Your Honor, but the woman knows the sentence will be execution if she is convicted. The fact that she still lives bears testimony to the fact that she desires to live, and, therefore, wishes to be found not guilty."

It was a reach, and Annie assumed everyone knew it.

The judge waved his hand dismissively.

"Defendant has entered a plea of not guilty. Given the threat to the public, no bail will be set, and the defendant shall remain in custody until such time a grand jury can be assembled and the court can convene. Counsel will review the docket and schedule trial."

"Permission to approach the bench, Your Honor," Carson said.

Griffiths waved his hand in invitation. Carson approached Griffiths and motioned for Sutton to join him. Despite the exclusivity of their conversation, it was fully within earshot of everyone there.

"Your Honor, it will be at least three months before the circuit brings us back to Weston to conduct a trial. Let us settle the matter now. Mr. Sutton has provided details concerning the defendant's arrest and charges. There is no reasonable way she could have committed these crimes, nor is there sufficient evidence to bring charges against her."

"She was discovered at the scene of the final murder and had clearly killed at least one of the victims ..." Griffiths consulted his notes. "... Mr. Harper—is that not correct?"

"Yes, Your Honor. However, Mr. Sutton here is her closest neighbor and was the first at the scene. He can testify to that evidence. This, combined with the description of the previous murders and, if nothing else, the stature of the accused, makes her no more a suspect than your own wife or daughters."

Griffiths looked over his glasses at Annie. Without further details, her size alone wouldn't acquit her, but she certainly looked nothing like the picture painted by the charges.

"Mr. Sutton, tell me what you found."

"Sir—Your Honor," Sam began, "Mrs. Hill did not commit these crimes. She is kind and caring, and—"

"Tell me what you found on the day of her arrest," Griffiths interrupted. "I do not mean to be brusque, but the circuit schedule is tight. If this is to be decided before late summer, I need something better than a character witness."

"I ..." Sam rebounded. "I found her and the two men—her husband and the other rancher—the morning after the last murder. She was holding a pistol. Mr. Harper lay a few paces away—he had been shot—and Mr. Hill was found behind some rocks further back with his throat cut."

Sam paused, and Griffiths raised his brows at him.

"Why does this lead you to believe she is not the killer?"

"It is true that she appeared to have killed Mr. Harper with the gun. The trauma of this has left her in a state of hysteria, as you can see." Sam gestured to Annie. "Also, Mr. Harper was wearing some sort of costume—with feathers—that had long claws—or knives—I do not know ... they were on his hands. Anyway, they appeared to be the weapon that killed Mr. Hill, and, from what I know of the other murders, no guns were used, but the other victims were cut open at the throat like Mr. Hill." Sam took a breath but then continued quickly as though afraid of being cut off again. "Harper's knives and Mr. Hill were covered in blood. Mrs. Hill had no blood on her. There is no reason to believe that she killed anyone but Harper, who had killed the other eleven people."

Griffiths pondered a moment. "How did you happen upon the scene?"

"I heard gunfire shortly before daybreak—my home is fifteen minutes away on foot—so I saddled a horse and rode down with a scattergun."

"What then?" Griffiths probed.

"I did my best to comfort Annie—Mrs. Hill—as she was the only survivor. She was unable to speak, so I pieced together what I could.

I had told my oldest boy to rouse my foreman, Campbell, if I did not return in an hour. When Campbell came, I sent him for the sheriff, who arrived at about noon."

"You will sign a sworn affidavit to this effect?"

"Yes, Your Honor."

"Be seated."

Griffiths addressed Schutz, Candon, and the other deputy, who confirmed the facts provided by Sutton.

"And it seemed reasonable to you, Sheriff, to arrest Mrs. Hill?" Griffiths asked pointedly.

The deputies withered under the question and looked to their boss.

"It did, Your Honor," came the tired reply.

Carson rolled his eyes, and Griffiths sighed in exasperation.

Schutz continued. "A dozen members of our community have been killed and mutilated in a manner that resembles an Indian attack, and now an Indian is discovered at the scene of the last attack …"

Sam's grinding teeth could be heard from across the room.

"Your Honor, we represent a community hell-bent on taking the law into their own hands. You know what is likely to happen to one condemned by popular opinion. You will remember, Your Honor, the incident with the Chinaman?"

"Enlighten the court, Sheriff," Griffiths said.

"Three years ago, a Chinese laborer was accused of killing a member from his own community in Weston's Chinese district. There was nothing but hearsay that tied him to the murder, and without sufficient evidence to charge him, he was released, only to be lynched a week later by a mob of townspeople who would never be named."

Griffiths leaned back in his chair, remembering the case. The man's real trial had been held without his knowledge—by self-appointed judges under the influence of whiskey in the dimly lit courtroom of the town saloon. Schutz's actions began to make sense. Weston had only grown since then, and every miscarriage of justice was pushing the people toward anarchy.

"Mrs. Hill's arrest was for her own good," Schutz concluded. "The likely killer is dead and cannot be tried. This is hard for those whose friends and family have been murdered. I cannot have their thirst for justice hijacked again by those with no respect for the law. Charges thrown out by the district court will mean more to the people than if no charges had been brought."

The mood in the room relaxed. It was as though the sheriff had been on trial yet stood acquitted by those whose opinion mattered the most. Maybe justice had a fighting chance after all—at least with the sheriff on its side.

"Mr. Carson?" Griffiths asked.

"Prosecution finds charges against the defendant insufficient."

"Charges dismissed," Griffiths replied with an air of finality, then, without acknowledging the triumph, the judge turned his attention back to Carson. "Next case."

CHAPTER TWENTY-NINE

Nita

So it was that Annie found herself acquitted by law yet condemned by her peers. Twice now she had escaped death—first at the hands of Ishkitini's usurper, then at the hands of her accusers—and twice she had considered herself alive only in body. Now, without ceremony, she found herself free, unclaimed by the reaper who had hovered over her for nearly two months. After her hearing, she was remanded to Sutton, who had agreed to see her safely home.

She sat silently in the wagon driven by Mr. Sutton, who seemed a little apprehensive. Even so, he spoke aloud as he drove.

"I have kept watch over the homestead and have cared for the livestock. I will have Campbell return your horses now or later—whenever you are ready. Besides the lawmen and Campbell, no one has set foot in your home since you left."

Annie caught only bits and pieces of Sutton's one-sided conversation. She had not expected to find herself in this situation—that was, alive—and her mind was working hard to make sense of it. She was certain that death, twice cheated, would soon be back for her.

During her stay in prison, she had entertained the thought of helping it along but soon rejected the idea. She had survived all this for a reason, and she would continue to fight—if only to honorably enter the afterlife. She was, however, gravely damaged and desperately lost. There was nothing for her here now; there was nothing for her anywhere. She had no family to return to. Even her government-allotted territory held no special meaning. She had her claim, but with Doyle gone, she was not sure if she could keep it. Besides, what could she do with it as one person? Run the budding little ranch into the ground? Sell and hope not to be swindled? She'd always be a murderer in the eyes of the public, so it made sense for her to leave the area.

Unfortunately, with nothing else to go on, she had to consider either marrying or supporting herself through prostitution. The fact that she had to even consider those prospects made her angry, and this was the first real emotion to pull her out of her numbness in what felt like forever.

She tended the little flame as she sat in Sutton's wagon, remembering what it was like to feel something. She remembered Harper's treachery, the men who accused her without reason, Doyle's unwillingness to let her in, the men who abused her and murdered her family so many years ago, until she was warm with emotion; a dangerous emotion, but emotion just the same.

By the time the wagon approached her homestead, she had made up her mind. This was her home, and she would stay. Let death come for her. Let the mob come and hang her from one of the scraggly trees. Let the true Ishkitini take her in the night. Let hunger or disease kill her in the winter months. Whatever befell, she would meet it head-on, stare it in the face, and scream in furious defiance until the soul was ripped from her body.

Sutton drove the wagon past Rebel Ranch toward his own home.

"Stop!" Annie blurted.

He jumped, and even Annie was startled at her own voice. It sounded strange. Sutton seemed uncomfortable with her request but obeyed anyway, pulling the reins and stopping short.

Annie slid from the wagon and stood on the side of the road looking up at her chauffeur. She gave a nod of dismissal as if to say "thank you," then turned and walked toward the house.

"Mrs. Hill—Annie—wait!" Sam jumped down and ran to catch her. "Annie!"

She turned and faced him.

"It is not safe for you to stay here. I have quarters for you on my property. Campbell can look after your affairs until we sort things out."

We. There is no "we." No, she would see this through on her own. And if anyone deprived her of life or liberty, she would deliver justice with the business end of a rifle.

"Annie ... it is not safe here. Come—"

"No."

Sutton opened his mouth to protest but was again cut off.

"*No!*" She shouted. She hated the way she was repaying his kindness, and that made her even angrier. Why should she feel bad for anyone? Hot angry tears began to swell. "*No! No! Nooo!*"

The fire was out of control, and her feelings, the anger, the heartbreak, and the fear all erupted in one massive outburst. She ran into the cabin, which sat cold and empty. She found Doyle's revolver on the table, replaced by Sutton after her arrest, and grabbed it. She rushed outside to face the shocked man.

"*Go!*" she screamed, waving the gun in the air. "*Go!*"

"Annie!" Sam shouted, trying to break her hysteria.

Annie breathed heavily. She gritted her teeth, and her eyes darkened. She leveled the gun at Sutton's chest and said in a trembling voice, "My ... name ... is Nita."

CHAPTER THIRTY

The Loneliness

Sutton dropped his hands and walked slowly toward the wagon, his movements belying his apparent fear that she would shoot him as he retreated. Climbing up into the driver's seat and taking the reins, Sam reached over and grabbed a sack of dry goods. Annie watched as he gently dropped them on the ground next to the wagon. She stared at him.

"A gift," he called out, "from John, the storekeeper."

Sutton couldn't be Annie's savior, and so, having done all he could, he slapped the reins and left Annie standing in the yard.

She stood alone in the dark cabin's main room. It was cold, uninviting, and uncared for. It was her heart in every way but broken. She shivered for as long as she could stand before building a fire.

"Small steps," she told herself. This would become her mantra.

When life was dark and without hope, it could only be a series of small steps. Build a fire, survive the night, eat tomorrow, cut firewood, check the cows—so on and so forth.

She would not go into town again—even if her safety could somehow be assured.

Until now, Annie had always believed there was someone she could rely on. Now, recognizing the foolishness of trust, she would not give it away again. She would live or die alone. If—when—she survived, it would be her own accomplishment. Food and water first, shelter second. No longer enough to protect her from wind and rain, her cabin now had to protect her from all earthly and unearthly evil. She remembered the nightly taunts of the owls as Harper had ravaged the countryside. Evil had followed her across this country, and, practical or not, fortifying her home was the best way to manufacture a sense of security.

Annie slept fitfully on the floor next to the fire until day broke. Along with her renewed sense of purpose, hunger had returned, and she gnawed at the bread from the sack John had packed for her. She pulled on a jacket and went outside in search of wood. Last night had been the first time she had been warm in many weeks, and it had felt good.

She spent a good portion of the morning chopping and stacking before finally deciding she had enough. She then turned her attention to the herd. They had been well cared for by Sutton's men and only had a day's neglect for Annie to make up. Her root cellar, likewise, was well cared for in that it hadn't been touched. If she could trap a rabbit every few days, she might have enough to see herself into spring.

Satisfied with the small steps of the day, she picked her way around the cabin, looking for weak spots. All at once, she rounded into view of Harper's old hut. She stopped short, staring, eyes wide. The hut stared back in the afternoon sun, an ugly reminder of a memory that she wanted nothing more than to erase. Her grip tightened around the revolver that she'd scarcely put down since arriving home. She breathed determinedly. She would not let this get the better of her. She walked slowly toward the hut, forcing herself to keep her breath steady.

"Mud and grass," she told herself. "I will not be haunted by a stack of mud and grass."

She stopped at the door, remembering the night she had burst through it in a panic, begging Harper—the destroyer of lives—to help her save Doyle—who refused to be saved. She pushed the door open and smelled—in her imagination, the stench of death.

"Mud and grass."

She would salvage whatever she could and use it to fortify her cabin.

During Annie's arraignment, Schutz had provided the court with details of what he and the other lawmen had found in Harper's hut. The head of William the cow dog, several locks of hair, and Asa Stanley's judgmental eyes. All this had been removed during the investigation. Schutz had granted temporary custody of Harper's valuables to Sutton, who secured them inside the cabin and appointed his most trusted hands to keep watch over the homestead in shifts, assuring them that Annie would soon be back for everything.

Annie, finding nothing of use in the hut, rested her mind just long enough to let the evil of the place register.

“What possessed this man?” she whispered. “What was he doing in here every night?”

Her head spun, and her stomach turned. She bailed out into the waning sun and retched hard, doubled over in the yard. She began to cry—deep ugly sobs—into the ground. It was all coming out. The unfairness, the anger, the sadness, the desolation. All of time, and the whole world, passed without notice as her grief-racked body emptied itself of all its pain on the cold desert earth.

“Why did I not let him kill me?” she shrieked. “Why did I not die with you, Doyle? What am I to do?”

She lay there, drained of everything but life, wishing to be taken. Slowly, quietly, in the afternoon dusk, her breathing became normal as her mind returned, and with it, her burning hatred of Harper.

CHAPTER THIRTY-ONE

Vengeance

The salvageable timbers and the solid door to the hut no longer mattered, nor did reinforcing her cabin. What mattered now, in the absence of vengeance, was defiance, desecration—anything to provide closure.

Annie feverishly ripped grass from the earth, grabbed kindling—anything that would burn—and stacked it at the entrance of the hut. She lit it and watched it spread. She continued to gather whatever was close at hand and fed the blaze. Soon the entire hut was engulfed, cleansing the earth, exorcising Annie's ranch, and bringing as much satisfaction as she was capable of enjoying.

Small steps.

Seeing the smoke in the distance, Campbell sent for Sam, who came running. They squinted at the fire below them in the distance. Seeing Annie's figure scrambling around and throwing more onto the fire assured them that she was acting purposefully and wasn't in any immediate danger.

"Your Injun woman is a lunatic," Campbell observed.

Sam turned and began walking back toward the house. "Would you not be, Camp? Grief does strange things to us."

Campbell shook his head and followed Sam. "It is good she is safe, at least. How long are you going to keep your eye on her?"

"Until I know she is safe, I will watch over her from whatever distance she requires."

After an hour, the fire began to die. Annie's energy flagged as the flames receded. She was exhausted. She turned and trudged wearily back to her cabin.

The unmistakable, blood-freezing shriek of the Ofunlo stopped her in her tracks and, in a moment, Annie was stripped of her satisfaction. She circled, looking everywhere in the fading light, pointing her revolver into the trees. Where was he?

She screamed. A terrified, angry, exasperated scream that echoed into silence. She screamed so loud her throat burned.

Nothing.

"What do you want from me?" she shouted. "What is there left to take?"

Her eyes landed on the door of her cabin, fifteen yards away. A second scream wrenched the night inside out. Annie dashed for the door, yanked it hard, and slammed it behind her. After throwing the bolt, she ran into the bedroom and threw herself into the farthest corner. All four guns, Doyle's Henry and Colt and Harper's matching set, were locked and loaded at her side.

The owl did not call again that night, but Annie could not sleep. Without a fire in the cabin, she huddled in the corner and shivered until, as day broke, she plucked up her courage enough to crawl into bed and cover herself. Finding some solace in the sounds of the morning, she finally drifted to sleep.

It was dusk when Annie woke. She lay still for several minutes, recounting the anguish of the day before and the terror of the night. She was still lost but also still alive—not yet a victim. She chided herself for panicking, for losing herself in grief, and remembered her goal:

Survive.

Stay alive.

Fully alive.

Rely on no one.

Steeling her mind, Annie told herself firmly that she would not be her own victim.

From now on, she promised, *if I become a victim, it will be only at the hands of another.*

Truly, she was tougher than most. Once the matter was resolved in her mind, she launched herself into action. There would be no more wasting away in her cabin while the cattle wandered.

Annie planned out what she would do to maintain her property each day and to make herself most comfortable and safe in the night.

She tidied herself because it felt familiar, then opened the door and stepped into the fading sunlight.

Small steps.

Annie worked quickly with the little daylight she had left. The animals were showing signs of neglect—particularly the horses, which someone had secretly returned the morning after she drove Sutton off her property. The cows, too, seemed more like prisoners. She remembered John's words from the night Doyle had nearly killed a man for calling her a savage.

"Evil begets evil."

It made a lot of sense now. There seemed to be no end to the evil Harper had visited upon the world. If even the cows suffered, what else was there that she couldn't see?

Annie did her best to make everyone comfortable in the corral as she continued to ponder. By the time she finished, she'd already dreamed up her second goal. She would change this place. She'd build a proper barn, for one thing. She would undo the evil that had been brought upon this desert patch. This was her ranch now—no, it would be a farm.

Annie exited the corral and rounded the corner of the windbreak. Come spring, she'd sell all but enough cattle to meet her personal needs, then turn her efforts to growing food. The river could be used to irrigate more land and—

She stopped. A huge bird watched her from atop the fence post. They stared at each other in the fast-setting darkness, neither moving, for a full minute. Annie felt the familiar panic rising inside of her. Was this finally the true Ishkitini? Had he waited patiently for her to take her life back so that he could take her soul now? It was unfair; it was *evil*.

CHAPTER THIRTY-TWO

Courage

THE OWL SAT UNBLINKING. Annie, tired of feeling like she had one foot perpetually in the grave, gradually became more angry than afraid. She reached into the deep pocket of her dress and felt the cool steel of the Colt.

She threw her shoulders toward her adversary in a mock lunge.

"Haah!"

Nothing.

So, it was a showdown. Ishkitini wanted her to lose her mind before he took her.

"Why have you come?" she shouted. "Have you not taken enough? Will you kill me too?" She drew the revolver. "Come and get me! Come on!"

The bird continued to stare her down but made no indication of fear or malice.

Enough of this!

She steadied her hand on her left forearm, aimed carefully, and fired. The cows started and moved uneasily to the opposite end of the corral. Annie's tormentor remained still for a moment, then neatly toppled off the post. Breathing heavily, she forced herself to walk boldly up to the owl and stand over his body. It was quite a shot, a clean kill.

It is just a bird, she told herself.

Her eyes wandered from the plumage to the curved cruel talons, the strong beak—a smaller version of what had lain in her husband's hands the night Harper had killed him.

"It is only a bird."

She nudged the body with her foot to satisfy herself, then picked the owl up by the feet like a dead chicken. She arched back and flung it into the night.

Let Ishkitini decide what he thinks of that, she thought defiantly as she strode toward the house. She brushed away a twinge of guilt at having killed without utility. She was no longer a naive girl; she now understood what drove people to kill. Maybe she would become like them. Maybe that would be okay. After all, evil begat evil.

Even so, dread surged inside her. What was she thinking? Would she become like Harper? Her nihilistic idea that life didn't matter made her feel powerful for a moment, but now she faced the revulsion that she could also become cold-blooded, killing out of anger and hate.

Stop! she screamed at herself. *Do not let yourself become a victim!*

Guilt and revulsion were products of weakness and had to be abandoned if she was to survive.

Once inside, Annie slammed the door and bolted it shut.

She built up the fire and forced herself to eat before turning to the evening task on her list—repairing her rabbit snares. She buried herself in the work, pushing the bitterness from her consciousness, but it seemed as soon as she forgot her pain, a thought or memory would break the surface to torment her again. It was exhausting. Ignoring her feelings was not endemic to her nature—that had been Doyle's thing—but with no way to resolve her heartbreak, no way to process her grief and move on, these emotions only served to threaten her survival. She had to push it aside. She had to focus on something—anything—else.

Eight-year-old Annie's hands ached from practicing the knots that her grandmother, Wiyot, had tried to teach her over the past week. The complicated assembly collapsed into a tangled mess in her fingers. She whispered a curse in her native tongue.

"No!" Wiyot warned.

"Pokni, it is useless. I cannot make it."

"You can and you will, Nita."

"It is no good."

"Do it again, just like I showed you."

Little Annie flexed her fingers and stretched her wrists. "Why must I learn this?"

"Because I know it. And if I know it, you must learn it. Every generation of ours loses knowledge, and so we must hold fast to what is within us—or we will lose ourselves forever."

"What will I do with a hawk?"

"You will keep a few of his feathers, then release him," came the unsatisfactory reply.

"Why do we—"

"So I can show you something else your generation does not know."

Annie looked at the old woman, pretending to mouth an unknown answer in hopes of enticing her grandmother to speak plainly. It didn't work. "We use them forrrr ..."

"Ceremonies, Nita. Sacred rites going back a thousand years—until now."

Wiyot stood up and shuffled off, muttering to herself irritably. Annie watched her irritably.

"Again!" Wiyot called from the kitchen.

Annie sighed, cursed—ever so quietly—and returned to her task.

Annie's hands worked tirelessly on her rabbit snares. When the memory cleared, she looked down at her work and discovered with some surprise that she had crafted the same bird-of-prey loop that had taken her so long to learn as a child.

She inspected it thoughtfully and pretended to wonder why she had done this. She already knew why; it was the same reason that old memory had surfaced in the first place. She could not let these birds continue to rob her of her sleep and security. She would hunt them down and litter her land with their bodies. She would either ward off Ishkitini or goad him into finally taking her off this miserable plane.

Folklore focused mainly on avoiding death at the hands of the monster, and Annie knew nothing of battling the supernatural. Truthfully, after shooting Ishkitini twice and only killing a man and a bird, she wasn't even sure how much of the legend she still believed. In her heart, she knew hunting owls wasn't a good plan. It was, however, something on which to focus her anger. All hate requires a demon, and Annie had appointed the owls to that end.

Annie set her snares the next day and checked them the morning after that. All eight were empty except for one.

Seeing the movement in the grass as she approached, Annie proceeded carefully, removing her knife from its sheath. A field rat writhed and gnawed at its leg, then froze as Annie drew near.

She knelt and inspected the animal. She noticed the rapid expansion and collapsing of the chest, its unblinking eyes, and the terror that covered it from nose to tail. Annie grimaced. She wasn't desperate enough to eat rats just yet, but she might later in the winter—time would tell.

She gave the knife a squeeze, disliking the feel of holding power over something so terrified, disturbed by the thought that she might kill it just to feel something. In one swift motion, Annie twisted the knife in her hand and rapped the creature smartly on the head. It lay back, stunned and twitching. She released the snare and collected the rat in her game bag.

That afternoon, she set her owl snare in the cabin's yard—just far enough from the house to make it appear safe and enticing but close enough to allow her quick access. She wired the rear paw of the rat to the snare and used rocks to box in the whole assembly. She stood back and looked at it doubtfully, then adjusted the rocks to force the desired angle of attack. It was not likely to work, but it was something on which to focus her anger. The trap would have to be sprung in a relatively short window before her rat chewed its leg off or some other nocturnal predator claimed the bait. She shrugged and went inside. If nothing else, she would inspect her trap the next morning and adjust her design as necessary. Even so, she kept the lantern close by as she slept.

Small steps.

That night, in the darkness, Annie was yanked awake by a commotion outside. Something had triggered her trap, and it was not happy. She had no idea what time it was, only that it was dark and cold. She lit the lantern, threw on a coat, stuffed the Colt in the pocket so she could undo the door latch, then dashed outside to see her trap being torn by Ofunlo. He was tiny compared to the white-faced bird she had shot two days before, but his ferocity more than made up for size.

Annie jammed her hand into the coat pocket for the gun, but it wasn't there. She swore as she patted the coat, searching for the weapon. The trap was starting to come apart now, and she knew she had to act fast. Stripping off the coat, she threw it over the bird to protect herself from the slashing talons and beak. She grabbed up her lantern and coat, complete with bird and the remains of the trap, and hauled the whole thing back into the house, noting the revolver at the threshold. It must have fallen as she fumbled with the door latch.

She slammed the door and threw the bird onto the table, grappling with it through the coat. Annie found the feathered mass, pinned it to the table, drew her knife—no sense in firing the gun indoors—and whipped the coat away.

Annie glared down at the little bird which had stopped struggling and now looked up at her, eyes wide, the little chest feathers heaving under the weight of her hand. She hesitated. It was so small, so powerless, so ... frightened—not unlike herself.

Annie momentarily relaxed her grip, and the owl, sensing an opportunity, renewed his struggle and pulled himself from Annie's wrest. His beak tore into the flesh of her hand, and she recoiled. Once free, he shot across the cabin, "hiding" in the corner of the far wall and ceiling. Instinctively, Annie hurled the knife across the room and buried it into the timbers inches from Ofunlo, who skittered away just in time. He clicked his beak in agitation.

"You wish to tell me something?" Annie forced out with mock bravado. "Let me hear you now!"

She was angry. This was, again, just a bird. The idea that she was just hunting birds was infuriating. It made her feel ineffective, powerless, and stupid.

She grabbed the revolver and went outside, leaving Ofunlo trapped inside the house.

"Where are you?" she howled into the night sky. "I have your messenger!"

She turned around slowly as if waiting for Ishkitini to appear. "What are you waiting for?"

Nothing.

Exasperated, she stormed back inside. Little Ofunlo glared at her from his corner; Annie glared right back. She flaunted the pistol at him.

"You belong to me now."

They spent the rest of the night that way, watching each other suspiciously, neither making a move to attack or escape, until Annie finally fell asleep at the table, gun in hand, while the lantern slowly burned out.

She woke with a start. Her eyes went immediately to the corner where she'd last seen Ofunlo. He hadn't moved. Annie closed her eyes and sighed heavily.

"What am I doing?" she asked aloud.

Ofunlo cocked his head and stared at her. Annie shook off her weariness and put on her boots. She locked her prisoner in the house and forced herself into her daily routine: checking her traps, milking the cows, ranging the herd, and watching, waiting for any signs of Ishkitini.

She returned late in the day to find that the owl had moved—and eaten. The remains of the rat, which Annie had left on the table with the remains of her trap, littered the far corner of the cabin. Ofunlo was nowhere to be found. Annie soon located him in the little bedroom, tucked, again, into a corner where the wall met the ceiling. He watched her prepare supper, making unpleasant sounds all the while.

Annie shot annoyed looks at the owl for audaciously taking up residence in her inner sanctum. The bedroom was sacred territory, and he was no guest. Doyle had designed the little bedroom in the cabin for their comfort. It was a luxury not afforded to most houses on the frontier. Having the little room that they could close themselves up in had brought much-needed comfort to them both.

Finally, having taken all she could stand, she grabbed a towel and went after him. "Out! Get out! Shoo!"

Annie whipped the towel at Ofunlo. He hissed and clicked his beak at her, but finally vacated the sacred place in which Annie then locked herself away with her dinner, pistol at her side.

Neither she nor Ofunlo rested well. He was a night bird and was irritable at being unable to hunt. Annie tossed and turned as her prisoner's constant flapping and whetstone-grinding sounds made it impossible for her to sleep for more than a few minutes at a time.

CHAPTER THIRTY-THREE

Softening

Annie was pleased the next morning to find that one of her snares had caught a decent-sized rabbit, and she immediately returned to the house to prepare it. Without much sleep to go on, a fresh meal by her fire now seemed so much more enjoyable than at the end of the day.

She cleaned and dressed it inside, enjoying the warmth from her reinvigorated fire. Ofunlo sat, tucked into his little corner, glaring daggers at her as she worked the knife. Annie rolled her eyes, and, after slicing a section of entrail, threw it in his direction.

The owl's eyes followed the chunk of meat as it landed on the floor beneath him. Annie watched curiously to see what would happen. Ofunlo suddenly moved farther down the wall, clicking his beak in ungrateful frustration.

Annie wagged the knife at him disapprovingly. "Do not push your luck, Ofunlo. I will cut that beak right off your—"

She caught herself, suddenly aware of how quickly she had gone from trembling in a corner to now having a conversation with this … thing, this representation of all the horror in her life. Where was Ishkitini? She had taken his little death-messenger prisoner, and he had done nothing. She had not gone mad like Harper; she had not been killed when the owls screeched. The sudden appearance of the birds late last year was uncanny …

But, she thought, *what if it was only coincidence?*

What if the barn owl on the fence post had just lost his home and resettled here, much like the Hills had done after the war? What if Ofunlo's arrival was merely a migratory anomaly?

What if Annie was wrong about all of it? What if the owls that preceded the tragedy in her village had just been easy to point her finger at? Perhaps they had always been there, unnoticed, ready to serve as scapegoats for the true evil that took her family away from her. What if she was guilty all along of the same judgment her neighbors now passed on her?

She felt as though she was waking up from a dream. She looked at Ofunlo thoughtfully, seeing him, for the first time, not as a prisoner of war, not as a symbol of death, but simply as a bird. A foul-tempered little bird.

He is stupid-looking. His giant head perched atop his little body. He was stupid-looking; but he was cute, too. He had become amusing to her, this fierce, powerless little cuss. In these moments, a creeping conviction finally surfaced in Annie's awareness.

She would not be Harper; she could not be Doyle. She cried when she hurt, she jumped when frightened, she loved deeply with abandon, and she forsook the hatred that others embraced. She was

Annie, and there was no need to be anyone different. Evil would beget evil no more. She didn't know where good and evil came from; but unlike Harper, she knew there was a line between the two; unlike Doyle, she knew that line had to be drawn by something greater than her own feelings.

She crossed to the door and opened it wide. Ofunlo blinked as the sunlight flooded the house. Annie backed away from the door and slowly approached the little bird. He clicked uncomfortably.

"You and I are done here. Get out."

He stared at her nervously, and Annie took a step toward him to force his decision. He sprang to life, and Annie jumped back instinctively as he shot across the room and out of the cabin.

Annie smoothed her dress, picked up Ofunlo's rejected scrap, and returned to preparing her breakfast.

CHAPTER THIRTY-FOUR

Spring

As if waiting for permission from Annie's heart, spring broke, and the ground began to thaw. Annie flung her efforts into planning crops. How much should she grow, how much *could* she grow, what could she fund after culling the herd in the spring?

No one had attempted to bother her during the winter, and she was hopeful that the population had accepted that she was not guilty of the crimes charged against her. It seemed unlikely that she should still be alive if the public was truly convinced that she had killed twelve members of their community. Still, she didn't know if her presence would awaken their vengeful nature, and for this reason, the prospect of doing business in town frightened her.

Each day, as she worked her patch of earth, she kept an eye on the road for Sutton. She needed to make amends with him if possible. After about a week of watching, she finally saw him driving a wagon and ran to hail him. Their last meeting had ended with him at gunpoint, so Annie, not really knowing what to expect, was encouraged when he pulled the reins and waited for her to reach him.

"Hello, Mr. Sutton," she said as she caught her breath.

"Hello, Mrs. Hill," he replied. "What can I do for you?"

Annie was grateful that Sam was so congenial, but, as her breath returned, so did her shame over the way she had treated him.

"Well," she began, "I suppose you can accept my apology for the way I have repaid your kindness. I am grateful now that you came to my aid, and I am sorry I behaved like a beast."

Sutton listened patiently, toying with the reins in his hand. "Call me Sam. And do not trouble yourself over it—it was nothing. No one should have to endure what you have been through, An—Nita, and I am glad to see you are doing well."

Annie was relieved. "I am doing much better, thank you."

"I would like to know what your plans are, though," Sam said cautiously. "You are clearly tough enough to survive, but what will you do besides that?"

Annie squared her shoulders. "I believe I will stay. I will farm."

Sam raised his brows, prompting Annie to explain.

"I will sell off all but three of my cows, and I will buy more chickens. I will build a proper barn ... and a fence—no more ranging—and ... I think I will irrigate more of my property."

She knew it was a lofty goal, and she could tell Sam was interested.

"And you will do all of this ... on your own?" he asked.

"It will take time," she admitted, "but maybe that is not so bad."

"Well," Sam began somewhat doubtfully, "please let me know if you need help. I have men available for hire and am happy to obtain supplies for you whenever I am in town."

Annie thanked him.

Sam looked uncomfortably at Annie, then asked, "Nita, I know you and Doyle were homesteaders, but tell me, did you ever obtain title to your land?"

"Doyle made an entry for patent as soon as he was eligible, but it is not yet ours—mine," she replied. It had not been something she had considered since Doyle died. The sudden realization that all her plans involved improving land that she didn't own made her sick.

"I had not thought of that," she added. "With Doyle ... gone, I do not know if I will be allowed to prove up."

"That is unfortunate," Sam replied bluntly. He grimaced. "This is likely not what you want to hear, but you may consider selling the improvements while you can and settling elsewhere."

It was more than unfortunate; it was bitterly unfair. Annie had every right to this land under the Homestead Act. By law, she was a US citizen, born to parents granted citizenship under the Treaty of Dancing Rabbit Creek. It was, however, a treaty that had been violated many times over and was now almost as lost to history as the cultural heritage her grandmother had instilled in her. She had been married to a white man, but he was a rebel, and now he was dead.

In life, there is law, and there is justice. Sometimes they are parallel, and sometimes not. Too often, even just laws are unjustly executed, and the fact of the matter was that Annie, though twice over entitled to the land she had sweated, bled, and cried upon for eight years, would likely never receive legal title to what was justly hers. She was a rebel-widowed Indian woman and, therefore, had fewer rights than most others in the country at that time.

She stood next to the wagon, crushed, watching the plans that had sustained her drive disappear into the realm of unattainability.

"What can I do?" she asked.

Sam fidgeted, clearly uncomfortable with the news he'd just laid on her. "You are not done yet, Nita," he encouraged. "I know people—good people. With your permission, I will look for a solution. However," he cautioned, "I suggest laying low for now—no big purchases, or inquiries into this matter. The worst thing you can do now is let people think your property is up for grabs."

This calmed Annie a little. She wasn't sure if Sutton could be trusted not to enrich himself at her expense, but for now, he was the closest thing to a friend she had. If she had any hope of staying there, she would have to extend a little faith to his character. She was Annie, and she believed in trust.

Annie thanked him. "I will be grateful for anything you can do."

CHAPTER THIRTY-FIVE

Proposal

Annie worked tirelessly to turn her ranch into the farm she wanted, pushing aside all discouraging thoughts. For now, this place was hers, and she would exercise faith that all would be made right in the end. Faith, however, cannot exist without the unknown, and despite her commitment, Annie, like most people, was anxious over that which she could not foresee.

With each passing day, she waited for news from Sutton. The weather grew warmer, and her little crops began to spring to life. At Sutton's request, Campbell had supplied Annie with fencing material which she used to protect her extended garden.

After several weeks, Sam finally called on Annie again. He hailed her as he rode up and, after tying his horse, walked over to the little field where Annie waited expectantly.

"Hello, Mrs. Hill."

"Hello, Mr. Sutton—Sam. What brings you by?"

"I have spoken with Carson, the attorney. He does not have all the answers, but he knows the law. More importantly, he knows what is right—regardless of what the law says. For this reason, I trust him. The matter is not simple, but there are two options that may work. One is easy, but will require you to move ..."

Annie scowled at this, and Sam quickly moved on.

"The second is a long shot, will take some time, and will require a lot of trust on your part. If it works, you will own your land outright. If it fails ..." He paused. "... I do not know what will come."

Annie let the preamble sink in for a moment.

"Tell me what you have found, and I will think it through," she said.

Sam nodded. "Five years ago, I applied for ownership of the land adjacent to you and am now eligible to claim title. If you are willing, I may be able to manipulate my application to include your land in my patent application. Campbell is willing to attest that Doyle worked for me and that the improvements—your cabin, the corral, the irrigation for your crops, and so on—are, in fact, my improvements. Once I am granted title, I will sell your land back to you for a sack of horse feed."

Annie followed the plan but could not digest the logic behind it. Anyone risking their own property to help her was too good to be true, and the prospect of giving Sutton everything she owned was scary. She wanted to extend trust, but she was not the same Annie who had married Doyle after a two-week courtship and who believed there was good in Harper.

Sutton seemed to understand the implications of his proposal.

"Nita," he warned, "you need to understand that proving up and obtaining patent is a very lengthy process. It also requires you to place a lot of unearned trust in my intentions. However, if you can trust me not to swindle you, it may be the fastest, most secure way for you to own your property outright."

He paused momentarily and watched Annie work a thumb over a chip in the blade of her hoe.

"The other option, then, is to sell your claim to me. I will ensure that you are paid fair value. I know it is not what you desire, but it is simple, efficient, and requires little risk on your part."

Annie liked neither option. She had hoped to be legally represented, to be defended to the land patent office, but it wasn't to be. What assurance could she have that Sutton, who would deceive the US government, wouldn't swindle her as well? If she sold for whatever Sutton decided "fair value" was, where was she supposed to go? What would she do? The thought of starting over from nothing was unbearable. Even if she did, what was the point if she couldn't claim land? Maybe Ishkitini, the destroyer of lives, did not exist in the sense she had imagined, but the evil was real enough, and it was intent on destroying her dreams, crushing her will, and robbing her joy.

It also occurred to Annie that as close to ruin as circumstances had brought her, it might very well be her lack of faith in Sam that would finish the job.

"I do not know what to do, Mr. Sutton," she said quietly.

Sutton adjusted his hat and looked out over the landscape. Unhindered by the flat terrain, a warm, constant breeze blew over them.

"I want to help you, Mrs. Hill, and I would rather you stayed.

Would it help if we split the difference?"

Annie looked up at him questioningly.

"I suspect you are wary of the power I would have if you were to hand your claim to me, but I can tell you want to stay."

She nodded softly.

Sam continued. "Suppose we have an arbiter determine a fair price for your improvements. Once we agree on terms, I will buy them from you, then hire you to keep working your property as you see fit. When I am granted patent, I will sell your portion back to you for the same price I pay you now. We will ask Carson to sign an agreement to that effect and enforce it on your behalf. At best, it gives you what you are entitled to. At worst, it pays you for what you and your husband built."

Sam was right. It was still a risk, but it was no riskier than her current situation—simply waiting to see if someone would force her off her property. She doubted even the worst case, being paid a fair price for the structures and livestock, would be offered by anyone else. It was the best she could hope for.

"At any rate, Nita, it is worth considering—"

"I will do it," Annie said. She drew herself up to full height. "I want fair value for every nail, and I want the same salary as the men who work for you ... and ..." She searched for the best way to finish. "... and you may call me Annie."

Sam smiled widely and extended his hand.

"Show me my new ranch, partner."

He toured the ranch with Annie, who showed him, with secret pride, everything that she had done to make the outfit viable. Sam remarked that she was quite adept at farming and encouraged Annie, telling her the idea of irrigating from the river was a wise move.

An hour later, as Sam rode off the property, Annie began to run after him. Throughout their conversation, Annie had tried to ignore her burning question, but she couldn't stand it anymore. She knew that if Sam was caught extending the boundaries of his claim on his patent application, it would nullify his own land claim. She had to know why he would risk changing the boundaries for her sake. Whatever was in the deal for him, she could not see.

Sam turned and rode back to meet her.

"Please." She panted. "I am grateful, but ... why are you doing all of this? You are taking a risk, and I cannot see the reward for you. Why, Sam?"

She fell silent, catching her breath and wondering if she'd unwisely questioned a good thing. But even if it was unwise, she had to understand how Sam's ideals drove him to act honorably yet also dishonorably.

Sam was quiet for a moment.

"I suppose, Annie," he began, "it comes down to this: I believe in God, and I believe what the Bible says about him. It says orphans and widows hold a special place in his heart, so I think maybe I should make room as well."

That was not what Annie had expected. The God she'd heard about would never say that.

"I have heard the Bible quoted, but never that," she answered. Then, without thinking, she added, "I have heard that it tells you to submit to your government."

As soon as the words were out, she regretted them. She had turned Sam's Bible around to insult his philosophy for kindness, a kindness she was receiving, no less. Her face burned. Sam, however, simply shrugged it off.

"There is good, and there is evil," he said. "Men have never fairly drawn the line between the two. I suppose I am no different."

He dismounted and stood on Annie's level.

"What is right is right, Annie, but this world—and everyone in it—is broken. Why else are we so often forced to choose between wrongs? None of our hearts can be trusted to decide what is righteous—but when I must choose between watching a widow's rights denied because of her color or cheating the very men who would deny her those rights, well ..." he sighed. "I must choose what is most right." Sam shrugged. "Honestly, Annie, the patent application process is so blatantly corrupt, I almost consider it a moral mercy to use that corruption against itself."

He climbed back into the saddle and looked down at her. "One way or another, we will keep you right here on your farm."

Weeks passed, and with them, so did Annie's anxiety. What did not pass from her mind, however, were Sam's thoughts on right and wrong, untrustworthy hearts, and choosing what is "most right." These were rocks in her shoes that she could neither ignore nor remove. Her thoughts led her in circles until, in frustration, she would cast the whole mess aside, only to have it creep back into her mind a short while later.

Annie allowed that trusting each man to determine what was right or wrong was problematic. If it wasn't, Doyle would still be alive, and Harper, well, who knew? Harper was a madman and either could not or would not do what was right. If a higher power, like Sam's God, granted authority to nations and bade his followers to obey their laws, then what? Even laws of nations were established by men who seemed only to answer to themselves. Men who, as far as Annie knew, justified their actions according to their god. Either way, it seemed that "right" depended entirely on who was in power.

As for herself, she had always done her best to be kind, trusting, and charitable, none of which she had seen from anyone in power. It felt wrong that someone—god or man—should simply decide they were more "right" than she. Before she knew it, she was right back to Doyle's conclusion that everyone should simply do what seemed right to them. Why did trying to decide what was good seem so evil?

Sutton sent hired teams to assist in building irrigation ditches for the farm. He assured the protesting Annie that he was merely protecting his investments through her alfalfa crops. The railroad had signaled the end of major cattle ranging operations, and each year it was becoming more practical—and profitable—to move toward a ranch that could simply breed and fatten cattle before shipping them out by train. Sam expected this investment to pay off by the time the federal government approved his application for title.

Annie began to enjoy the company of others once again. There was never any shortage of workers, and Campbell, who had warmed to her, made sure that her directions were followed to the letter.

Annie found she rather liked managing the operations and used the relief from hard labor to provide whatever comfort she could to the hired hands through food and drink. Her simple, beautiful nature—as Doyle had so often called it—was returning, and she quickly won the approval of those who worked for her.

CHAPTER THIRTY-SIX

Last Strike

Harper's burned-out hut still blighted the homestead, an ugly scar by day, a hulking silhouette at dusk, and always a reminder to Annie of the man who had killed her husband and nearly driven her to madness.

Out of respect for the widow's grief, no one had dared mention anything about it to her, but the day came when she finally decided to tear it down. She was now strong enough to approach the building again. Removing the structure completely would be healing.

Annie used a horse and tackle to pull down the walls and roof, then went to work with a mattock to spread the remains over the dirt until there were no traces left. She was prying up the floorboards when she disturbed a nest of rattlers. She leapt back just as the largest snake struck out at her shins. The snake recoiled, and Annie swung the mattock hard, catching the snake on the head and stunning it. She quickly chopped the head from the body as the rest of the snakes crawled away.

"How fitting that this awful place should be a haunt for vipers," she said aloud to herself.

She stomped and beat the ground in an effort to drive away anything else lurking in the floorboards before going back to work. She had to see this through.

Annie continued pulling the boards up and was surprised to see a substantial cavity underneath them. It was as though Harper had built a little cellar after moving in. In the last corner of the void, untouched by the flames Annie had set that winter, lay a stack of parchment bound together as a book. Annie took a deep breath and reached for it.

Fangs sank deep into her hand, and she cried out. The snake had not even sounded a warning before striking and now held on to her hand as she jumped back and tried to shake it off. It clung to her, coiling around her arm, working its teeth deeper into her flesh, burning her with venom. The more she flung and shook her arm, the tighter her attacker coiled. It rattled furiously at her. Annie tripped over a board and fell hard, her head snapping back onto the packed earth and dazing her.

"God!" she screamed in delirious wrath, "when does it *end?*"

A burst of energy whizzed before her eyes, slamming into her arm and pinning it to the ground. She jerked and tried to pull away, but she was held fast. Talons gripped around the serpent's body and dug into the flesh of her arm. She screamed in terror against the deafening rattle of the snake. The beak snapped, and feathers flew. Annie felt sick; she was losing consciousness. As her vision went, she heard the unmistakable screech of the Ishkitini.

Annie was aware of being helped to her bed, of vomiting, of shaking uncontrollably, but little else. She drifted in and out with no concept of time. A woman she didn't know tended to her.

In her dreams she saw Harper, as Ishkitini, lurching toward her. Enormous birds dove at him, slashing him with their talons as he swung at them with his claws. She would wake briefly, sweating and muttering, before sinking back into the same dream. Again and again it happened, Harper slashing, owls attacking, feathers flying, shrieking, screaming, over and over and over until she could not take it any longer. She flew at Harper, cursing him, beating him, and attempting to rip his mask off. She ripped the feathers from his face, and as her hands wrapped around his throat, Annie suddenly realized she was no longer fighting Harper; this was the true Ishkitini.

"Why have you come for me?" she shouted. "What are you?"

They lay there, eyes locked, breathing heavily. With a low gurgling sound, Ishkitini opened his mouth.

"I am your fear, and you have made me strong."

CHAPTER THIRTY-SEVEN

Camber

Annie awoke. She blinked hard and looked around her little room. For the first time in days, her mind was clear. She lifted her bandaged hand and flexed it. It hurt and was still a little swollen, but she was fairly certain that most of the poison had left her system.

The snakebite is real, but what about the rest of it? The way it held me? What about the bird? Was it all delirium?

A woman bustled in, interrupting Annie's thoughts.

"Annie, you are awake!" she exclaimed. "I thought you were too far gone!"

The woman quickly fetched tea, which Annie drank tenderly.

"I swear, I have never seen a snakebite like that." The woman indicated with her head toward Annie's hand. "Nor a reaction like yours. Sammy had the doctor come day before yesterday, and he has now called for the preacher, although it looks like you no longer have need of him! Well, not for rites anyway."

"Thank you," Annie said. Then added, "I am sorry, I do not think we have met."

"No, we have not," the woman replied, "although it is a pity that this is how we should meet. I am Madeline Sutton. Sammy is my husband. I have heard so much about you and am glad to finally meet you."

Annie felt a little bad for not knowing Sutton was married.

"I have been caring for my father back East," Madeline continued, "since late last year and only returned last week ... and now, here I am, caring for you!"

"It is too kind," Annie said, "but thank you."

"I am at my best when I have someone to take care of—just one small reason I am glad you are recovering."

Annie managed a smile.

She rested comfortably throughout the day. Maddie, as Mrs. Sutton insisted she be called, was clearly working hard not to be overly chatty.

That afternoon, there was a reverent knock at the door, and Maddie answered.

"Hello, Reverend Camber," said Maddie in a cheery voice.

Annie strained her ears.

"Hello, Mrs. Sutton," a quiet voice replied. "How is Mrs. Hill?"

"You will not believe it, but she is making a full recovery!"

"Thank God for miracles," he said. "The way Sam talked, I was certain I would be too late."

"Well, Sam was right, but she has really come to. Come, talk with her."

Maddie appeared next to Annie's doorway and ushered Camber, dressed in minister's clothing, into Annie's bedroom. The tall man ducked slightly and removed his hat as he walked through the doorway.

Annie smoothed her bedclothes nervously. *Why is a preacher here?*

"Annie, Reverend Camber has come to call on you."

"Hello, Mrs. Hill," said Camber. "I cannot tell you how relieved I am to hear you are doing so well!"

Annie nodded appreciatively. "Thank you."

"My name is Paul Camber, and I am a minister ... as you might have guessed." He tapped the collar around his neck. "The Suttons know me well and asked me to perform your last rites. They did not realize how tough you are, I suppose."

Annie smiled again. She felt good. A little trembly, but good. Only now, learning how close she had come to death, she was not yet sure what to make of it.

"You do ... this, a lot?" she asked, making a haphazard sign of the cross to indicate blessing.

"When asked." Camber smiled. "I really am glad I do not have to perform rites over you today. I know what you have been through—Sam has kept me updated. There has been much prayer over you these last several months, Annie."

Annie toyed with the bedclothes, wondering whether prayers had anything to do with her being alive.

Maddie brought in a chair from the kitchen, and Camber sat. "Thank you, Maddie."

He waited for Maddie to leave before turning to Annie. "I spoke to your husband shortly before his death—in town—he was there with ... well, with Harper, I think."

Annie stared through the cabin wall. The memory of Doyle seemed distant now.

"He did not speak much, but he seemed kindhearted if not a bit—"

"Sad," Annie finished for him.

"Yes. Sad."

"You are right," Annie replied, still staring through the wall. "He was kind, but he was always a bit sad."

"Of course, I knew about the three of you," Paul said, "from talking to Sam. Although, he said you kept quite to yourselves."

"We did. That was Doyle's way ... and Harper's, I suppose."

Camber looked up. "Mrs. Hill, I do pray a lot, but besides that, what can I do for you?"

Annie searched for something intelligent to say. Suddenly, she remembered her conversation with Sam about choosing what is most right—and how it had annoyed her so. This man probably couldn't help, but she wanted to at least ask his opinion on the matter.

"Can you tell me," she began, "where righteousness comes from?"

No, she thought, *that is not what I mean*.

She tried again. "If God ..." she stopped. This was frustrating. How was she supposed to put it all into a simple question? "Doyle was a good man," she blurted, "a *good* man! Harper was evil, and I

... I do not know what I am." Annie floundered in a sea of wordless thoughts. "What is good, what is right? And who dares decide for the rest of us?"

She wondered if she'd gone too far, spewed too much for this man of God to handle. What if he couldn't explain how his God was just? She sank into her pillows. She was still weak, and it hadn't taken much to wind her.

Camber exhaled slowly and closed his eyes as if in brief prayer.

"Well," he said carefully, "I can tell you what I know—which is only a little—and I can tell you what I believe, and what I try to do with it all. Perhaps it will be helpful." He paused. "I know that there is good and there is bad, things like pleasure and pain, but I do not trust my knowledge much further than that. However, I do not think it is quite that simple. I believe in God, the God of the Bible, and I believe what the Bible says about him. The Bible says that 'right' is defined by God and no one else. It has to be this way—one authority and no other—otherwise, we must accept that everyone is free to do as he wishes."

Annie listened intently, waiting for the magic idea that would solve her confusion. She was pretty sure this wasn't it. "Doyle thought everyone should do what he thinks is right."

"I know." Paul smiled, then quickly added, "When I met your husband, he mentioned this to me."

"And what did you tell him?"

Camber hesitated. "I asked him how that had worked for him."

Annie breathed out slowly. "I suppose we know now. Doyle felt that no one else could be trusted and I am certain that is how Harper was able to take him down."

Paul leaned in reassuringly. "Perhaps, but perhaps not. Absent Harper, Doyle would still be here, yes?"

"In body, at least," she replied miserably. "He was so withdrawn toward the end I do not know how much of his spirit remained."

"As for Harper," Camber continued, "there may have been, at least at some point, some moral code to which he held himself accountable. But whether our nature makes us kind or unkind, we must be accountable to someone besides ourselves. Otherwise, who can stand?"

He was touching the pain in Annie's heart.

"That is what I cannot bear!" she cried. "A God who will draw a line that no one can hold, men who draw lines so that only they may stand, and the rest of us all caught in the middle."

"That is unbearable, Annie," he said. "But God does more than draw a line. He holds that line for us. Our efforts to be righteous are just acts that show our love for him—and for each other."

Annie wasn't convinced. "It is unfair that Harper, the murderer, was no more punished than Doyle, who did his best. What does your God say about that?"

"He hates it," Paul replied.

She hadn't expected that. She looked over at him.

"Justice means everything bad is punished and everything good is rewarded, would you agree?" Camber asked.

Annie nodded in agreement.

He held out his palms as if they were scales. "This is human justice. The problem is that justice is not always served, and most cannot agree on what punishment is just for which crime. God's justice is different. He says, 'The wages of sin is death.' This means all sin, not just the worst ones. It also means we are all bad and true justice would kill us all."

She already knew she didn't like that. "Do I deserve the same death as Harper?"

Camber leaned in toward Annie. "Jesus satisfied the penalty of death that justice demands, Annie. He holds the line for us. When we accept that gift, then our evil is removed, and we are made good. Instead of punishing us all, God's justice rewards us all. Because of that, he hates that Harper and Doyle and the Stanleys and so many others died."

Annie gritted her teeth. "Only Harper should have died."

Camber sat back and raised his brows. "Oh, that would have been far better for us," he allowed, "but when? Before he killed Doyle? Before Asa? When the murderous thoughts first entered his mind?"

Annie's head was beginning to hurt.

"What about when he was a child?" Camber asked.

"I do not know," she confessed.

"You have heard of Jesus?"

"I know stories from school," she answered.

"You and Doyle were betrayed by Harper; Jesus was also betrayed by a friend. When a woman lavished Jesus with perfume, many of his followers thought this wasteful and wrong, but only one spoke up, only one would not let the matter rest, and only one—the same one—delivered Jesus to the people who murdered him."

This story was familiar. She'd heard it as a girl at the territory schools she attended.

"Jude?" she asked, hesitantly.

"Judas, yes," he replied.

Annie looked the preacher in his face. "And you believe all of this?"

"I do."

Annie wasn't sure how this translated to the world she knew. "So, Jesus died ... what happened to Judas?"

"He also died."

"It is still unfair," she said.

"I would say so," Camber agreed, "but you already know the world is unfair, and does not follow the laws of justice. Even legal title to your property hangs by a thread."

Annie shot him an alarmed look. "You know about that?"

"Sam trusts me, and I believe in what he is doing. On our side of eternity, sometimes there is right; sometimes there is only less wrong." Camber sat back in his chair. "All I can say is trust in God to tell you what is right. Do right whenever possible; and when not possible, do the least wrong. It really is as simple as that."

"You make it sound so simple," Annie said.

"Well," Camber said. "Things are usually more black-and-white than most are willing to admit, but we are blanketed in a gray fog.

Keep hoping for the day when wrong will be erased and right will be easy. Until then, accept that sometimes the difference between the masses and the maniac is only a decision away."

Annie nodded her head quietly and stared into the wall.

Camber smiled. "I can see you are getting tired—and you need your rest. I will go talk to Maddie for a bit."

He stood and picked up his hat and Bible. Reaching the door, he turned as though an idea had just occurred to him.

"Here," he said, "take this." He held out his Bible.

Annie looked from the old, worn book to Camber's face. "Are you sure?"

"Yes. I want you to have it—as long as you are on bed rest. You can return it to me when you are back on your feet."

Annie yawned as Camber set the book on top of another on the table beside her bed.

"Goodbye, Mrs. Hill."

Annie awoke several hours later to find the Bible next to her bed on a small table. She picked it up and read the note Camber had tucked in the pages. Underneath the Bible lay the crudely bound book she had found under Harper's hut. She marveled that the Bible, Sam and Paul's guide to truth and justice, had sat atop Harper's writings—the journal of a madman who had abandoned all justice in the fog of his moral desolation.

CHAPTER THIRTY-EIGHT

Healing

"There I was," Campbell said, looking from Sam to Maddie to Annie, "helping repair the fence—about a hundred yards from Annie when I heard her scream. I could tell right away that something awful was going on, but nothing could have readied me for what I saw."

He paused for dramatic effect.

"Oh, go on!" Maddie yelled. Then, to Annie, she said, "He *always* does this. The man cannot tell a simple story!"

Annie giggled despite herself and put her bowl of potatoes down on the kitchen table.

"I look toward the old hut—where I last saw her—and I see her" he swung his right arm in a wide and frantic circle "—slinging her arm around like this. Only there is something attached!"

"It was the snake?" Annie asked, leaning forward.

"Yes! So, I run to help her, but before I can get there, this ... little bird ... dives out of nowhere and joins the fight. I thought it was attacking her at first, but then I see it pinning her arm down and trying to ... to ..."

Campbell broke out in a laugh. It was a contagious laugh, and in a few seconds, all four of them had tears running down their faces. The story, which had once possessed a sinister nature as Annie lay dying, suddenly seemed utterly ridiculous.

"I just ..." Campbell gasped, trying to recover. "What possesses a bird to *do* that?"

Maddie held her side until her laughter subsided. "Oh my! I... cannot ..." She snorted, then burst into another fit of laughter.

"And ... and ... and the best thing—" Campbell gasped, "was that after it ripped the snake off of Annie's wrist, it tried to carry it off ... but it could barely carry the cursed thing!"

Sam almost spewed his coffee.

By the time the last fits of giggles subsided, Annie's face fairly ached.

"Tell me," she asked, "was it ... a little saw-whet owl?"

"So you *do* remember it!" Campbell said.

Annie hadn't seen anything of the owl but a feathered ball of energy—and even then, she had been dazed from the blow to her head. But Campbell's response told her that her rescuer was none other than the obnoxious, foul-tempered little Ofunlo she had released from her cabin so many weeks ago. Annie now realized, finally and fully, that the demon messenger of *Ishkitini*, whom she had blamed for all evil, the little demon she had attacked and imprisoned was at worst a silly bird; at best, he was ordained to *deliver* her from evil—whether by pulling the teeth from her hand, by providing a sign that she was not alone in her suffering, or both.

The nightmare was reduced to nothing, and she was free.

Maddie relegated Annie to bed rest for a few more days. During this time, Annie read Camber's Bible as much as she could stand. She enjoyed learning the details of the stories she'd heard as a girl, but the language and context made it difficult to follow. In this way, it was both captivating and irritating.

Maddie was no stranger to the Book and helped her new friend through many of the initial questions. This, combined with her confinement to the cabin, led Annie to put more effort into reading the Book than she otherwise would have cared to spend.

Camber's note suggested she begin with the book of Romans, and after ignoring it, starting at the beginning, and quickly being bored to tears, she followed his direction and began reading about how God and the Bible applied to her. No longer alone, Annie would come to rely on her people—Maddie, Sam, Paul, and others—to help her understand this book, what it said about good and evil, and why any of it mattered to people here below.

By the end of the week, Annie had almost completely recovered, and she now had her cabin to herself again. Alone, she finally turned her attention to the other book—the one she had wanted to read but didn't want to explain to anyone. As painful as she knew it would be, she had to read it to at least try to make some sense of the senseless.

She pored over Harper's scribblings, putting together the disjointed thoughts and filling the gaps with what she knew of his past. It took some time, but Annie eventually was able to map out the descent into madness that Harper himself had missed. She saw the boy whom no one else had seen. A boy denied justice and love. The man who craved both. Who mislabeled his actions as just and who finally gave himself over to his desires.

This would have been too much for the old Annie. The new Annie, however, was armed with people who cared for her, the knowledge of a God who loved her, and the fearless courage that naturally followed.

Over time, Annie would come to know a peace that would allow her to forgive Harper. It wasn't immediate nor would it be without reservation, yet it would be all the same miraculous.

Epilogue

Somewhere Above, the Owl Screamed

Over the next two years, Annie continued to finesse her irrigation farming experiment. Though not overwhelmingly successful in its first year, she gained enough improvement with each successive season that Sutton was able to cease ranging his cattle and fully feed them with the alfalfa they harvested.

Annie hired men through Sutton Ranch to assist her in trenching irrigation lines to water her crops and other large projects. Her acquittal of the murders was enough to insulate her from mob reprisal but not enough to make her universally welcome in Weston. The fact remained that her husband's friend was a killer—although putting an end to Harper's madness did redeem her in the eyes of many. Annie accepted this. She had her friends and she belonged to a God who loved her.

Capitalism has its virtues, and as more and more people conducted business with her and with Sutton, more and more people came to recognize that Annie was not who they believed she was.

A few short years into growing her farm, Sutton reported to Annie that he had been granted full title to both claims.

"I am prepared to pay back your purchase price," Annie said immediately, "plus fair value for all the improvements."

"I am sorry, Annie, we cannot accept your offer," Sam said in a grave tone.

Maddie squeezed his hand.

Annie stifled a twinge of panic. She trusted the Suttons, but this was unexpected.

She drew herself up. "Then what is your proposal?"

"Mr. Carson has drawn up our proposal," he said, indicating for Carson to hand over the document.

Carson, stone-faced, handed over an official-looking paper, and Annie began to read, skimming over the legal jargon about "parties hereto referred to as 'Hill' and 'Sutton.' " Finally, she came to the terms of purchase and stopped.

"One sack of the finest horse feed?" she asked.

The Suttons came apart at the seams.

"This is not funny, Sam," she protested, but she was wrong. Soon, she, too, was laughing. She loved how joyful these people were.

Carson smiled and shook his head at the antic. "Yes, very clever." He checked his watch. "If there is nothing further ..."

"Wait!" Annie shouted, "I wish to counter the proposal."

Carson gave Annie a bewildered look.

"What more could you possibly—"

"In addition to your demands," Annie said, addressing the Suttons, "I will provide a deep discount on all produce purchased from my farm over the next ten years."

Sam laughed heartily. "If that is your demand, then we reluctantly accept."

"Oh, Annie, you are too kind!" Maddie said, hugging her.

Carson produced a paper and pen and began taking notes. "I must say, I have never officiated a contract wherein each party's main concern was the benefit of the other."

Sam slapped Carson playfully on the back and knocked his glasses askew. "I am sorry our joke is at the expense of your tight schedule."

Carson smiled and shook his head. "Think nothing of it, Sam ... it is good for my soul."

Annie smiled until her face ached. She was finally free—from fear, obligation, and the threat of legal injustice. She owned her own property and now had the resources to hire workers to help her maintain her growing farm.

One summer evening, Annie and Maddie were walking from the Sutton Ranch back to her home when an owl screeched over them, causing them to jump and forcing a startled yelp from poor Maddie. Annie laughed at her embarrassed friend and remembered how she had been frozen in fear by the same sound for most of her life. She pointed Ofunlo out to Maddie.

"Hello, little one," she said in a deliberately unfriendly tone.

Ofunlo made his little hissing sound and clicked his beak from above, then swooped off to hunt.

"For the life of me, I will *never* get used to that." Maddie shook the startled look from her face. "Honestly, I do not know how you sleep with these blasted owls screaming at you all night."

They stopped at the entrance to Annie's farm, under the sign that read "HFO." Annie beheld it with satisfaction, remembering how Sam and Carson, when drafting legal documents, had asked

Annie what she planned to call her farm. She had considered a moment before answering.

"It has become a haunt for owls. That will serve as a name."

Sutton and Carson exchanged looks, and Carson, who had no patience for cleverness, simply put "HFO." Sutton had the initials hammered out for her and installed in an arch over the entrance to her property.

"I think folks are calling it 'Hill's Farming Operation,' " he said after presenting the gift to her.

"I will take that over 'Rebel Ranch' any day of the week!" she had countered.

Annie now turned to her friend. "I used to hate it more than you could know, but ... I do not mind it so much anymore."

Then you will understand what is right and just and fair—every good path. For wisdom will enter your heart, and knowledge will be pleasant to your soul.

Proverbs 2:9–10

Acknowledgments

Thank you to everyone who helped get this story off the ground:

To Ross Johnson. Without his creative mind, this story never could have been.

To Sarah Billington-Bautista who provided the first editorial review for my manuscript.

To Ray Brock and Martin Pool for pushing me to think bigger than a short story on my hard drive.

To Rodrigo Frias for his mentorship, support, and for encouraging me to never stop writing.

To all the friends and family—too many to list here—whose financial and moral support made it possible to share this story with the world.

To the staff and partners of Redemption Press, who walked me through the process of polishing and publishing this story.

Thank you to my brilliant kids, who put up with my foul moods and helped me remember what true creativity is.

Thank you to my wife, Julie, for her twenty-plus years of encouragement and support in all my creative endeavors, her quiet strength, and her simply beautiful nature, which inspired Annie's character in this story.

About the Author

Matt Posey is an inspirational speaker, writer of redemption stories, and constant recipient of God's grace and forgiveness.

He enjoys carpentry—particularly taking old, worn-out items and creating something beautiful from them. He calls this "redemption carpentry."

Matt lives in northern Utah with his wife, Julie, his two children, a small cat, and a large dog.

Order Information

Additional copies of this book can be ordered
wherever Christian books are sold.

Printed in the USA
CPSIA information can be obtained
at www.ICGtesting.com
CBHW030347101124
17131CB00003B/13